AND JUSTICE FOR NONE

The Life and Death of An Innocent man

By

Mary Ann West

And Justice for None," by Mary Ann West

Reg. U.S. Copyright by Mary Ann West, 2000

ISBN: 978-1-4303-0896-6

Published 2006 by Barshoe Books,
P.O. 6452
Edmond, Oklahoma 73083-6452.

All rights reserved. No part of this publication may be reproduced, stored in a retrieval system, or transmitted in any form or by any means, electronic, mechanical, recording or otherwise without the prior written permission of Mary Ann West.

Manufactured in the United States of America

AUTHOR'S NOTE

This is a work of creative non-fiction. The events are based on state and federal court records, newspaper reports, the Congressional Record, interviews and personal knowledge of the community. Only where indicated by * have pseudonyms been inserted.

In 1988, two men were arrested and charged with the rape/murder of Debra Sue Carter, a twenty-one year old woman in Ada, Oklahoma on December 8, 1982. These men were Ronald Keith Williamson and Dennis Leon Fritz. My son-in-law was court appointed to defend Dennis Fritz. This case, he told me, was an interesting one and he encouraged me to write about it.

My husband had been a state court judge in Ada, prior to his appointment to the U.S. District Court in Oklahoma City. We lived in Ada for fifteen years and knew everyone connected to the legal profession there. Because of the lapse of five years between the murder and the arrests, the lack of evidence and the drama of exhuming the body of the victim, the trial provided much local as well as state interest. However, the jury convicted both Ron Williamson and Dennis Fritz. Williamson received the death penalty and Fritz was given a life sentence.

I put the manuscript away.

End of story, I thought.

However, on April 14, 1999, my daughter called me and asked if I still had my manuscript from the 1988 trial because both these men were being released the next day. DNA evidence had proved their innocence.

The following account pieces together the twenty-four years that it has taken to put to an end this tragic story of justice gone wrong.

INTRODUCTION

On September 20, 1994, Ronald Keith Williamson, 38, paces the double locked 6'x8' cell. He has been on death row for seven years. The once blond hair of this former baseball player for the NY Yankees hangs in long gray strands over his thin shoulders. Most of his teeth are missing. He is 6'2" tall and now weighs less than 120 pounds.

He seldom sleeps. Night and day are indistinguishable on death row. When awake, he screams his cries of innocence. The sounds he makes must be loud enough to drown the loudspeaker into which the guards take turns shouting, "This is Debbie Carter", they taunt, "why did you kill me.....kill me..... kill me…"

"I didn't kill you, Debbie Carter," his raspy voice wails, "I am an innocent man."

Ron Williamson's execution is scheduled for 12:30 a.m., September 27, 1994. His sister is sent a form to select a funeral home to receive his body.

Normally, the State sets the execution date 60 days in advance of the execution, but in Williamson's case the time is reduced to 30 days. His appellant attorney is caught short and works feverishly to draw up a brief to present to the federal court requesting more time. This is Williamson's final plea.

On September 22, 1994, she hand delivers this brief to the State Attorney General's office. The document reaches the desk of U.S. District Judge Frank Seay, Chief Judge of the Eastern District of Oklahoma that same day.

On September 23, 1994, Judge Seay issues an Emergency Stay of Execution five days – less than three working days – before Ronald Keith Williamson's scheduled death by lethal injection.

Almost one year later, Judge Seay orders a new trial. His order is prefaced by the following statement:

"While considering my decision in this case I told a friend, a layman, I believed the facts and law dictated that I must grant a new trial to a defendant who had been convicted and sentenced to death.

My friend asked, 'Is he a murderer?'

I replied simply, 'We won't know until he receives a fair trial.' God help us, if ever in this great country we turn our heads while people who have not had fair trials are executed. That almost happened in this case."

ACCORDINGLY, the Writ of Habeas Corpus shall issue, unless within one hundred and twenty (120) days of the entry of this order, the State grants Petitioner a new trial or, in the alternative, orders his permanent release from custody.

IT IS SO ORDERED this 19th day of September, 1995.
Frank H. Seay
U.S. District Judge

After the Emergency Stay of Execution was ordered in 1994, Ron Williamson was transferred to the prison hospital and placed under the care of a psychiatrist. This psychiatrist made periodic reports to the court regarding the inmate's mental health while the defense prepared for the court ordered retrial.

In a letter to the court from Dr. Charles Grundy, the doctor assigned to Williamson, stated: " I have interviewed Mr. Williamson on several occasions since he entered the hospital. In general, his symptomatology appears to be exacerbated. His speech is pressured and loud. It appears that he has developed psychotic symptoms, evidenced by delusions of grandiosity and ideas of reference. For example, he recently informed me that a television reporter was going to assist in broadcasting information about his case throughout the world. He spoke as if he knew this television reporter, alluding to the belief that his special status of importance would allow him beneficial treatment from the media."

On April 15, 1999, Ronald Williamson was released from prison. DNA testing proved his innocence.

When Williamson was filmed walking into the small Ada, Oklahoma, courtroom, several reporters ran alongside him, film crews from NBC, ABC, CBS, cameras on their shoulders shouted, "How do you feel this morning?" the reporter asked.

"I feel just fine this morning," Williamson replied, and then he smiled broadly into the lens of the camera that would broadcast his picture and this story throughout the world.

CHAPTER ONE
Tuesday – December 6, 1982

> "I been
> in an out
> o' them
> ole honky tonks
> for twenty years
> but I ain't
> never seen
> the likes
> o' her in
> one of 'em.
>
> Why, she looked
> like she walked
> right out of a
> store window."
>
> Bedrock
> Images From The Wayside

It's a bright, sunny afternoon, warm with a south breeze. Debra Carter rolls down the window of her car and lets the wind whip her long brown hair around her face. She's smiling. Her grades are great this semester. The proof is in the blue notebook on the seat beside her.

She's having a birthday party on Friday at her own place. It's her night off from her part time job. The guys are bringing beer. Her friend, Gina, promised snacks. She adjusts the rear view mirror so she can see her face. She smiles at her reflection. Her teeth are straight and white and her blue eyes sparkle. "Twenty-one," she says aloud, "and moving on."

Debbie is on her way to Sears to buy curtains for her new garage apartment. She wants the white cotton ones with the lace ruffles she saw there last week after she rented the place from Marie Simpson* who lives across the street and owns several rental properties in town. Marie is a friend of Debbie's family.

"You're sure this is ok with Charlie?" Marie had asked when Debbie came to look at the apartment. "I'm not doing nothing without Charlie knowing about it."

"Dad's fine with it," Debbie answered, although she hadn't talked to him yet. "I turn twenty-one next week. I think he's glad to get me out of the house." She smiled at Marie.

"Well, I had to get a new refrigerator," Marie said, "after the last folks moved out. The stove has new top burners. I'll give Charlie a call. You're still a kid – to me anyway."

They were at the top of the stairway on the landing. Marie put the key in the door. The room contained a couch, coffee table and a chair.

"That was my mother's chair," Marie said. "You remember her. She used to baby sit you sometimes."

"Sure." Debbie answered.

"Most of the furniture in here belonged to her. Charlie was a big help to us when she died. A lot of folks were. 'Course, living here in Ada is kind of like living in one big family."

"I've never lived anyplace else."

"Me neither. I'll talk to Charlie tomorrow."

That night Debbie told Charlie about the apartment. "It's really neat, Daddy. Marie showed it to me. Furnished too. Has a new refrigerator and the stove has new top burners."

"Somehow I can't see you getting much use out of that kitchen stove." He smiled at her. "Besides, it's not exactly in the silk stocking part of town."

"Come on, now." Debbie laughed. "Since when have any of us Carters lived in the silk stocking part of town?"

Charlie smiled and shrugged. "It's not that I don't trust you or anything, it's just that you're my baby girl."

"Aw, Daddy, I'm all grown up – remember twenty-one next week and earning a living, too."

"And that's something else – working in that bar at night. It's not what I had in mind for you to be doing."

"It's good money though," she reminded. "And don't forget I'm going to school and paying for most of it too."

"I think me and Peggy interfere with your social life." He winked at her.

"Maybe you do, but Mom's a lot more tolerant. Anyway, it's not the social life so much, it's that I want to be on my own. And besides, we're all right here in Ada, Oklahoma – God's country. Why, you're not more than a couple of miles from that apartment on 8th street."

Charlie nodded. "Tell you what," he said, reaching for his billfold, "business has been good this year. I just got the bid on the brick work for that new office those lawyers are building downtown, so you take this credit card here and go get whatever kind of curtains and stuff you need for that new place of yours." He handed her the card. "Under one condition."

"What's the condition?"

"You have to invite me to the housewarming."

Debbie hugged him. "Did I ever tell you that I love you? Quit worrying so much. I've got a lot of good friends here and I've got you – and Daddy, I'll let you in on a secret. I like living here in Ada and I'm going to live here for the rest of my life."

CHAPTER TWO

"You tell me of urban agony,
of alienation and loss of identity.

And I answer:

You have not seen the
carcasses of gentle victims
after years of picking and tearing
by wanton vultures
that nightly roost
in the better homes
of small towns"

                      Bedrock
             Images From The Wayside

    The country club in the community of Ada, Oklahoma is an imposing compound. The greens are immaculate, trimmed to perfection and a difficult eighteen holes to play, the members are pleased to inform strangers. The club building is low and rambling, the lounge furnished with deep, leather sofas and the brass lamps have fashionable black shades. Heavy, burgundy drapes border the high windows and the tables are mahogany – solid wood and polished. The sun-room which travels the length of the building, is filled with white wicker furniture and soft cushions patterned in yellow daisies. The pool beyond sparkles in the sun and reflects the light, as might a well-cut diamond.

    However, to order a drink from the white-coated waiter or from the bar, a member must have remembered to bring his own whiskey, labeled with his name and left on the shelf behind the bar because Ada is in a dry county and the law is strictly enforced.

    Each November, a drive is started by the "wets" to repeal the law and each November a petition is circulated by the "drys" through the churches and endorsed by the ministerial alliance, against repeal. For many years, the question has appeared on the ballot and every year, the "wets" lose to the "drys" by an overwhelming margin.

    Oil money built Ada.

While most of the country stood shivering in line for free soup during the 1930's, Ada became the site of one of the largest and most productive oil finds in history and the community and its residents prospered. Jobs were plentiful for the residents without land and the mineral rights beneath the surface, but for those residents who owned that land and those minerals, life was sweet indeed.

The homes those owners built were palatial with acres of manicured lawn bordering paved driveways to the entrances. Located south of the business district where sycamores and oaks grow tall and the evergreens are lush year round, the area became known as Kings Row.

All in all, the economy provided income for most of the residents. The rich employed the poor who spent the money they earned to make the rich richer. And although the poor never became rich, they never stood in the soup lines, as did their big city contemporaries.

The population of Ada during those oil boom years increased to something over fifteen thousand residents and has remained stable to this day.

Ada had a lawless beginning.

The original settlement known as Daggs Flat in the 1890's, consisted of a few small dilapidated and dreary stores. The name was later changed to Ada after the eldest daughter of an early day merchant, Jeff Reed.

In 1888, a forward thinking young man, Tom Hope, established the first bank in Ada. A barbeque was held on the opening day of this bank with invitations sent by Hope to every rancher within one hundred miles. Chickasaw Governor Johnston of Tishomingo was invited along with all members of his tribe. The food was ample. Quail, turkey, squirrel and rabbit in addition to the beef Governor Johnston provided graced the long tables. The Corner Saloon provided several five-gallon barrels of whiskey.

During the celebration, a horseman rode up to the hitching rail in front of the bank. His name was Gus Bobbitt, a U.S. Marshal.

"Don't you know that it's illegal in the Indian Territory to give away liquor in the Chickasaw Nation?" he asked Tom Hope.

Hope poured a cup of whiskey for Bobbitt, who sampled it and graciously agreed that small violations could be overlooked on special occasions. The two men shook hands and later in the day

Bobbitt deposited several thousand dollars in the new bank for the U.S. government.

There was no municipal government in Ada, I.T.(Indian Territory), no police officers except for the Chickasaw Mounted Police who were without authority and were in town only once a month. However, there was a great deal of piety in evidence. Six churches were already established. The Masons had a lodge as well, with more than one hundred members. Gus Bobbitt was one of those members. Mrs. Hope organized a Ladies Study Club that met in the homes of the members and discussed the works of Lord Tennyson, Whitman and Emerson. As tea was served to the well-dressed ladies, random pistol shots could be heard and the shouts from the cowboys echoed in the distance.

There was good money to be made in the whiskey business, both in distilling it and selling it. Several saloons operated in town. One proprietor who was also the bartender said that he didn't like the job. "There's too much dodging of bullets to suit me," he complained. "Them pistols are always going off in all directions."

Since there were no laws in place, the territory was filled with outlaws, cattle rustlers and the "Indian Skinners" who were land sharks who took advantage of the Indians to acquire their homesteads for paltry sums. Most of the county judges were bribed by these men and word got around that Ada was the place were the courts were easy and juries were reluctant to hang or even sentence to prison cold blooded killers.

The Masons and Gus Bobbitt were trying to change this situation.

By 1907, when the Indian Territory became the State of Oklahoma, Ada had over five thousand residents. Three banks were located there, two weekly newspapers, one daily paper, a cottonseed mill and an ice factory. Telephones and electric lights had been installed and a huge cement plant was under construction. Train travel had become commonplace with three railroads coming through town.

Civilization was coming with statehood, but the outlaws weren't happy. Joe Allen and Jesse West began to make arrangements for the murder of Gus Bobbitt. They believed that with Bobbitt gone, they would be able to take over the town and rule without interference.

Allen and West went to Ft. Worth, Texas and hired a man named Jim Miller, a hired gun, who had eliminated more than fifty men. Miller would be paid two thousand dollars for the job.

Bobbitt, unarmed, was in his wagon on his way home from town when Miller ambushed him. The shotgun blazed twice and Bobbitt died instantly.

If Miller had met Bobbitt on the street with both of them armed, and shot it out face to face, not much would have been made of it. The spirit of the Old West was still alive in that year of 1909, and leniency to a slayer was available if both were armed, but since this was not the case, the citizens, especially the Masons, were angry.

Rumor had it that Miller had killed the famed sheriff, Pat Garrett, the officer who killed Billy the Kid. He had received fifteen hundred dollars for that job and now the Masons raised two thousand dollars as a reward for his capture.

The next week Miller was captured in Ft. Worth and returned to Ada to stand trial along with West, Allen and Berry Burrell who had recruited Miller. Miller wasn't worried. He was confident he would be released because he made another arrangement with a prominent lawyer, Moman Pruiett, to pay ten thousand dollars for his services.

Pruiett, who had yet to lose a case, told a friend that this was his "Big One".

But Pruiett was wrong because forty Masons were gathering on April 19, 1909.

At 2 a.m., these men marched in pairs down the street toward the jail where the four accused slept peacefully. It was not a mob, but a disciplined group of men on a mission for justice. They carried ropes and bailing wire. From there justice was swift.

The four men were marched to a livery stable about thirty feet from the jail, ropes thrown over the rafters and the legs of the men tied with the bailing wire. The nooses drawn around the four necks were tightened as, one at a time, they were hauled into the air.

The news of this lynching became national news and the nation was outraged by this act of violence, but the nation did not understand how much Ada had endured from the laxity of the courts which permitted murder for a price.

The bodies of these men were left hanging for several days. Telegrams poured into to Ada from Texas, New Mexico and Arizona congratulating the citizens for freeing them of Jim Miller who had terrorized their own citizens for years.

The promised investigation by Governor Haskell never materialized and the Masons vowed never to mention the affair as long as any of the participants were living. Moman Pruiett, who was in Oklahoma City, expecting to go to Ada the next day for the trial and had been paid ten thousand dollars to defend the four heard the news, called the bellboy and said, "Send me up a quart of whiskey. I just lost four clients down in Ada."

The historical museum in Ada devotes space for this infamous event in its history. The photographs of the four men hanging in the livery stable are prominently displayed, as is an open Bible with the marked passage "An eye for an eye."

Ada became, and is a cultural community. The influence of Mrs. Hope and the study clubs still exist. The names have changed and the members rarely discuss Lord Tennyson, but they remain a part of civilized society.

East Central University, which borders Kings Row, has a lovely campus and the President's home, with its white columns and green lawn is not unlike Margaret Mitchell's Tara. The school sponsors a little theater group and the writer-in-residence program is recognized statewide. Although the chairman of the Art Department has a national following, many of the ladies who weekly meet for bridge at the Club, consider him to be eccentric since he wears his graying hair in a pony tail and entertains his students, mostly male it is rumored, at his home on the outskirts of town

Ada boasts that 90% of the population is on the church rolls. There are fifty one churches within the city limits, forty-nine of them Protestant, one Catholic and one gathering of Mormons who meet in the homes of the members, but rent and maintain a small apartment for the young missionary boys who occupy it on a rotating basis.

Actually, it is a wonderful place to live – if, of course, you happen to be rich and white and married and a member of the Baptist Church.

By 1982, the oil boom of the late 1970's had enveloped Ada. Once again oil created a sense of prosperity that had not been seen since those years in the 1930's.

Farmers and ranchers were receiving as much as three thousand dollars an acre just to lease the minerals under the land they owned. And those who found themselves with pumping wells on this land were cashing monthly checks in the amount of thirty thousand or more.

The influx of oil field workers in the community brought young men coming from depressed areas of the country for hard work and high salaries. They looked for housing, girls and a good time. The search for housing created a building boom. Mobile home sales skyrocketed. And the girls were there too.

The search for good times created the Coachlight Bar and many others like it. And, the Coachlight provided jobs for girls like Debbie Carter.

Located outside the city limits, the building stood on a hill with access to the highway by way of a gravel road. Pink and green neon lights outlined the roof and the name COACHLIGHT BAR was spelled out in the same colors, blinking on and off in alternating intervals. In daylight, the building had a barn-like appearance hardly distinguishable from other buildings visible from the highway, but at night, it could be seen for miles.

Inside, the bar was centered along the longest wall. It was complete with a brass rail, scattered bar stools and behind it a mirror with scenes of flat land dotted with oil derricks painted in silhouette with a background of long, thin clouds in orange, indicating either sunrise or sunset, depending on the viewer's imagination.

Tables and chairs bordered the dance floor. A half dozen pool tables located toward the back of the room had low hanging lights above them making their green surfaces bright, causing them to appear suspended in mid-air against the dark wall beyond. During the week, music came from an amplified sound system, but on Friday and Saturday nights the music was live and loud and produced by a five-piece band hired by Harry Palmer*, the owner. Harry paid them three hundred dollars a night plus all the beer they could drink.

Although there were some fights – mostly over the affections of a girl – Harry saw to it that confrontations were kept to a minimum. Harry didn't want any trouble. That's why he located the Coachlight, with it's pink and green beckoning lights, just outside the staid community of Ada, and barely over the county line where liquor was legal and there was not a church steeple to be seen.

CHAPTER THREE

On the night of December 7, 1982, the unseasonably warm weather signaled a change toward colder temperatures. The Coachlight closed at 1 a.m. on weeknights, and 2 a.m. on Friday and Saturday. By midnight there were still a dozen or so customers. At one of the tables sat several young people. On the table were two paper plates filled with nachos sprinkled with jalapeno peppers. An ashtray held dozens of cigarette butts plus three or four still lit. The smoke rose in straight lines before flattening into cloud like circles above the heads of the smokers.

Debbie and her friend, Gina Vietta, took turns waitressing at the two "working stations" in the club and sometimes tending bar. The atmosphere was casual. Near closing time, the girls could sit and visit with friends – smoke and rest a bit after a busy night.

Debbie was sitting at one of these tables just after midnight. Gina was behind the bar polishing glasses and finishing up prior to closing. Debbie wore a red, western cut shirt with the cuffs turned up and jeans. A leather belt with her name DEBBIE carved into it was threaded through her belt loops. She was wearing white, canvas shoes and white cotton socks knitted with ribs for a soft springy feel around her ankles.

"Hey, Gina," Debbie said, motioning to her to join her at the table with their friends, "It's closing time. Come sit over here."

"In a minute," Gina said as she put the last of the glasses on the shelf in front of the mirror behind the bar.

A young, good-looking man sitting at the bar, waved to Debbie and pointed to an empty bar stool next to him. She waved back, but continued to sit at the table.

Tommy Glover, who had worked with Debbie the summer before at the Brockway Glass Company, was at the table. He finished the last of his beer and leaned toward her. "Dance?" he asked.

"Sure," she answered as they stood up and he pulled her close. The music playing was a melancholy country/western song – something about making my brown eyes blue.

The man at the bar walked toward them and tapped Glover on the shoulder. Glover backed away and shrugged. When the man's back was to Glover Debbie mouthed the words, "save me".

December 8, 1982

In the afternoon, when Charlie Carter tried to call Debbie and the line was busy, he thought little of it. "Girls", he said to himself, remembering all the times he tried to call home when she was living there and the line would be tied up. But, after several calls and later in the day as well, he tried calling her at work.

"Haven't seen her," Harry Palmer said. "Not like her to be late, but she'll show," he added. "Deb's good with the customers."

"She likes that job, Harry. I know you're watching after her."

"She's a good kid. Smart, too. Quit worrying about her. She's probably out there shopping. Said you were helping her fix up that new place she rented."

Charlie smiled. "Think I'll ever see that credit card again?"

"Probably not." Harry laughed.

Charlie tried Debbie's number again – still no answer. He called the operator to check the line.

"There's no voice sound," the operator said, "receiver must be off the hook."

Marie Simpson's twelve-year old daughter and her daughter's best friend who lived next door there on 8th street, always walked home from school together. The girls usually saw Debbie outside about this time of day. They met her when she moved into the apartment. They knew she went to college part time and worked nights at the Coachlight. The girls thought she must have an exciting life and speculated about what it would be like to be independent and have their own cars and an apartment.

Because of the snow on her car, they knew she had not been to class that day and were envious of an adult world in which there was no punishment for class absence.

"Look at the snow on Debbie's car."

"I'll bet she didn't go to school today."

"I wish I could just go to school when I wanted to."

"I think she has a boyfriend."

"I wish I had a boyfriend and a job and if I didn't want to go to school I just wouldn't go!"

Marie opened the door and the girls rushed inside. "Hurry up, girls. It's cold out there. There're cookies in the kitchen."

"But, Mama, we want to play outside in the snow."

"Warm up first. I made hot chocolate."

The girls sat at the kitchen table, still wearing their coats.

"I don't think Debbie went to school today, Mama. Her car's all covered up with snow. And I think I saw her door open a little."

Marie rented her apartments on an 'all bills paid' basis and had a policy of not interfering with her tenants, but with the weather change and an open door could mean the utility bills would cost her some extra money. She picked up the phone and dialed Debbie's number. The line was busy. She knew Charlie kept in close touch with his daughter, so she tried to call him, but he didn't answer.

The girls finished their hot chocolate and rushed outside.

Marie put the cups in the sink and looked out her kitchen window. The girls were trying to build a snowman with the inch or so of snow that had fallen. Then she noticed Charlie's car parked there by Debbie's car. She got her coat and went outside. The sun's reflection on the snow was blinding.

About the time she reached the bottom of the stairway leading up to Debbie's apartment, Charlie opened the door and stood on the landing for a few seconds holding the stair rail. She could see that he was shaking as he gripped the rail and his face was ashen.

"What's wrong?" she shouted up to him.

The girls had stopped their play and were standing, motionless, looking up at him.

"Is Debbie all right?"

Charlie shook his head.

"Go call an ambulance!" she told the girls. "Hurry!"

"It's too late," Charlie said flatly. "There's no need for an ambulance now."

By the time the police arrived, a crowd had gathered. Charlie Carter was sitting in his car.

It was a quiet crowd, made up of people in nearby homes and apartments. They stood, hands in pockets, coat collars turned up against the cold and whispered softly to each other as the police filed up and down the stairway.

Marie called Peggy and then she went back outside and walked over to the car where Charlie sat and asked if she could do anything else. Charlie shook his head. Then she called to the two girls and told them to go inside her house. They did, reluctantly, but stationed themselves at the kitchen window for a full view of Debbie's apartment.

Dennis Smith, the detective from the Ada Police Department, was the first to enter the apartment. The sun was below the horizon and the temperature dropped with the disappearance of the light. The apartment, too, was dark and Smith felt for a light switch, but carefully with a handkerchief in his hand.

As soon as he found the switch, an overhead light flooded the room. A large chair was on its side, couch cushions and clothing were on the floor and the television was smashed. The kitchen, at one end of the room had a sink, refrigerator and a small, free standing stove. A chrome and Formica topped table with two matching chairs filled this space. There was something red smeared on the table with words written on it.

The bedroom door was open and with the same handkerchief he touched the light switch. The bed had been pushed against the closet door and the nightstand turned over. A lamp with its ceramic base broken was beneath an overturned cedar chest. Some white, cotton curtains were still partially attached to the curtain rod, one end of which remained fastened to the wall. The remaining part of the curtain was beneath the body of Debbie Carter who lay face down, her nude body smeared with something red on the back of her thighs and down her legs. There were words written on her back with this same red stuff.

A belt was around her neck. It was a leather belt with the name DEBBIE carved into it. She wore socks, white cotton ones knitted with ribs around the ankles.

Smith leaned closer. The red stuff that covered her legs, he realized, from the sweet, sour smell, was catsup and the words on her back spelled DIE BITCH.

Then he lifted her slightly off the floor by one shoulder. He saw that a washcloth was stuffed in her mouth. He gasped and released her quickly because her eyes were wide open, staring blindly at whatever horror was the last thing Debbie Carter ever saw.

CHAPTER FOUR

On December 8, 1982, at 6:30 p.m. Fred Jordan's phone rang. He was in the shower. His clothes – dark suit, white shirt, and conservative striped tie – were on the bed. The dinner he would attend that evening honored a prominent public official and was being held at the Petroleum Club high atop the Liberty Tower Building overlooking the Oklahoma City skyline.

Dr. Jordan was tired. He had done three autopsies that day. The first, an old woman beaten and raped by an intruder in her home, the next a transient, dead several days and discovered in an abandoned building, and the last, a child of three-abuse with head trauma. The children were the worst. Even after eleven years as the chief medical examiner for the State, he dreaded those most.
He straightened his tie and reached for his overcoat in the hall closet. It was snowing outside and windy. Then his pager beeped. The number was his answering service. He reached for the phone and dialed.

"There's been a murder down in Ada," the voice said. "We tried to call you."

"Didn't hear the phone."

"Body's going to the funeral home there. They'll get it up here in the morning. Keep her in cold storage overnight."

"Right," he said, "anyone we know?"

"Don't think so – young girl – last name Carter. Pretty they said. Or was."

"Sure." He answered.

"Have a good evening," the voice finished.

He drove slowly on his way downtown. The windshield wipers cleared the wet snow with even strokes. He was in no hurry. All his patients could wait for him. Nobody dies twice.

The autopsy Dr. Jordan performed on Debbie Carter was routine. He was training an assistant, but the assistant was young and Jordan wanted to start this one off right. The assistant before had passed out before the Y cut was made and the skin flaps flayed back.

Any surgical procedure can be grisly, but dissections are worse. As he made the cut he remembered the first autopsy he witnessed. It was another young woman, not much older than the one on the dissecting table. That woman died after a lengthy illness of heart disease. When the assistants tried to pull her from the steel table to the dissecting table her skin stuck and she had to be wet down with a hose in order to release her. There was no concern regarding bruising, or any kind of tenderness that would happen in a surgical operating room. In fact, the dissecting room was located in the basement, hidden behind a storage area. The walls were peeling paint. The tile floor sloped toward an open drain under the table.

After the first few autopsies, surgeons become detached from the person. The procedure requires attention to the details of anatomy. As Jordan cut through the rib cage and lifted it as he might the hood of his car, he looked at the face of Debbie Carter. In spite of the bruises on her face and neck, she had been a beautiful girl.

He dictated his findings into a tape recorder as he examined the internal organs. There was extensive internal bruising and bleeding and deep inside her rectum, he discovered a metal catsup bottle top. Uncharacteristically, he paused and shook his head. Whoever did this was not only angry but he was vicious, intent on humiliation.

His report told a story of defensive wounds to her arms and upper body, major cuts inside her mouth and cheeks and puncture wounds on her face and neck. She was raped and sodomized. The victim, he said, had put up quite a struggle for her life.

CHAPTER FIVE

Detective Dennis Smith interviewed more than twenty men who were reported to be regular customers at the Coachlight. Hair and saliva samples were taken from all of them, including Ron Williamson, who said that he was at home by 10 p.m. on the night of December 7th, Dennis Fritz who said he wasn't at the Coachlight on that night, Glen Gore who insisted that he knew Debbie Carter only slightly because they had been classmates in grade school, and Tommy Glover who said that he had seen Glen Gore talking to Debbie Carter in the parking lot as she got into her car to drive home after the bar closed.

Blood, hair, semen samples and fingerprints were taken from the apartment where Carter was killed. The hair samples came from the stuffed animals Debbie kept on her bed, the clothing she wore on the night of the murder and the washcloth stuffed in her mouth. There were hundreds of hair samples to be analyzed and these were placed in an ordinary kitchen type plastic bag. A section of the bedroom wall was removed because it contained a bloody palm print. This wall section was carefully encased in brown paper.

The Parkview Café in Ada was located on Main Street west of the railroad tracks. Ryan's New and Used Furniture Store and the Acme Feed and Seed were on either side of this twenty year old restaurant. Across the street was a small park with playground equipment and a wading pool, shaded by tall oaks and sycamore trees. There is no major highway through the city of Ada, so the traffic is slow and parking on the street is permitted. The Parkview, a gathering place for the usual crowd of early morning coffee drinkers, were there the morning of December 9th. The aroma of frying eggs and sausage mixed and mingled with the cigarette smoke. The topic of conversation was the discovery of the murder the day before.

"Rough crowd out there at that bar." The older man, dressed in overalls that buttoned over his shoulders and covered a red flannel shirt, said to the younger man who sat across from him and puffed on a cigarette.

"When you start mixing all that liquor and dope together, there's bound to be trouble," the younger man said. "I heard the police already have a list of twenty guys."

"Ron Williamson's one of 'em. Top of the list, I'd guess."

"Ronnie's about as crazy as they come. Been at the state hospital up there in Vinita in the loony ward a dozen times, I've been told."

"Hell of an athlete though." The old man poured a little of his coffee into the saucer and sipped it. "Best baseball player even seen in these parts."

"Damn right. Remember when he got drafted by the Oakland A's?"

The old man nodded. "In about '73 or '74, I think. I know it was before he married that girl who won the Miss Ada beauty contest."

"I heard he got cut from the A's because of his temper."

"He was always mean to fight."

"Used to call up the coaches and complain about things not going his way. Anyway they got rid of him."

"A' course the New York Yankees hired him for their farm club down in Florida, and it might have worked out for him, too, if he hadn't had trouble with his arm – he was a pitcher, you know."

"Is that the reason they let him go?"

"That's what I heard, but Ronnie being as hard to get along with as he was probably didn't help him much."

"That girl quit him, too, didn't she?"

"You can see why."

The old man sighed. "Hard to live with somebody like Ronnie – crazy as he is and mean to boot."

The younger man leaned across the table. "I remember when he moved up to Tulsa and he got in some trouble with the law up there. Got charged with rape."

"Goddamn."

"Nothing ever came of it, but that's when he moved back here to Ada."

"I heard he lives with his folks."

"It's been hard on 'em."

"Goddamn. A rape charge, you say."

After the breakfast crowd cleared out, the waitress, Agnes, who had been employed there for ten years, handed the last of the dishes through the kitchen window behind the counter to the cook.

" I think the folks here in this town are planning on a hanging."

"They don't hang anybody anymore," the cook said. "The last hanging took place back in the sixties when those two fellows killed that Cutter Family up in Garden City, Kansas. Took 'em almost twenty minutes to die by the rope."

"How'd you know that?"

"I may be a cook, but I'm not ignorant, Agnes. I can read, you know."

"Twenty minutes, you say."

CHAPTER SIX

Ron Williamson had been treated for mental illness since 1979. He was diagnosed as displaying behavior indicative of Schizophrenia, Bipolar Disorder, Borderline Personality Disorder and Paranoid Personality Disorder.

Williamson, no stranger to the court system, had been arrested on a bogus check charge and placed under house arrest in the late 1970's. He promptly escaped. The judge in that case officially adjudged and decreed that Williamson was unable to appreciate the charges against him. He was also unable to consult with his counsel or rationally assist in his defense. The court further found that he was a mentally ill person, based on the findings of Dr. Charles W. Amos, who had evaluated him prior to his arrest. Further, Dr. Amos indicated that he was delusional and recommended that he be transferred to Eastern State Hospital for evaluation

This trip to Eastern State Hospital would mark the beginning of many such evaluations.

In December of 1979, the Mental Health Department of St. Anthony's Hospital in Oklahoma wrote: "Actually, this boy has demonstrated rather bizarre and sometimes psychopathic behavior. Whether he is manic as the counselor in Ada thought, or a schizoid individual with sociopathic trends, or the reverse, sociopathic individual with schizoid trends may never be determined. Long term treatment may be required."

From November 3, 1980, to December 15, 1980, the Mental Health Services of Southern Oklahoma observed Williamson. Initial Diagnostic Impressions: "Alcohol addiction and unspecified drug dependence."

Williamson spent three months – from November 16, 1981 to February 11, 1982, at the Mental Health Services of Southern Oklahoma. When he was discharged, his prognosis was suicidal ideation. They recommended anti-depression drugs and more psychotherapy.

Ron Williamson was the youngest of the children in the Williamson family. Their father was a salesman, sometimes going door-to-door selling home care products.

The children were Annette, Renee and Ronnie, as he was called as a child. Annette frequently took the roll of caregiver when her mother was working.

In the affidavits taken from these family members, Annette said, "Ronnie was an exceptionally bright child. He was big for his age and well liked by his teachers and friends and, early on, had a talent for sports, especially baseball, which he loved. He could be a "show off" and demanding, but we thought that was because of being the youngest and a boy, of course.

Our parents were determined to help him with his baseball career and when Ronnie was a senior in high-school they moved to Asher, Oklahoma, a town about thirty miles north of Ada, so that he could complete his senior year there because of that school's outstanding baseball program. After he graduated, he went to Bacone College, near Muskogee, Oklahoma, and played baseball there. After only one semester, the Oakland Athletics drafted him for their farm club in Coos-Bay, Oregon. The A's gave him a signing bonus of sixteen thousand dollars. He was the highest draft pick in Oklahoma that year. Ronnie was so excited that he went out and bought expensive presents for Mom and Dad.

The real tragedy is that Ronnie might have been as good a baseball player as his hero, Mickey Mantle, who was also from Oklahoma, if he hadn't had trouble with his arm. When Ronnie was in high school, he even set up a kind of shrine with all of the Mantle paraphernalia that he could find. Ronnie was a kind of star athlete hero then. He dated the prettiest girl in Ada, Patty O'Brian, who won the title of Miss Ada, in the preliminary Miss Oklahoma pageant. Ronnie and Patty were married after he joined the Oakland A's, and she stayed with him for some time, even after he was dropped from the team and his mental condition became such a problem.

Our mother was in her thirties when she carried Ronnie and she slipped and fell during this time. When he was four or five, he fell out of a moving car and hit his head on the pavement. He didn't appear to be injured, so mother didn't take him to the doctor, but I remember that he complained of headaches as a child.

I think the loss of his baseball career led to his frequent hospitalizations in various mental institutions in the state. Sometimes he would cry uncontrollably and after his marriage ended he was hospitalized several times, but strangely enough, the attending physician wouldn't talk either to my mother or me about the reason for his treatment.

He lived in Tulsa for a time, but he had trouble keeping any kind of a job. Twice he was tried for rape. He was acquitted both times, but these rape trials were so traumatic for him that he moved back to Ada and lived with our parents most of the time. He would sleep twenty hours a day and he insisted on sleeping on the living room couch because he thought there were snakes in his bedroom. After our father died, Ronnie's aberrant behavior caused out mother to spend the night away from home on many occasions, however, she would never say why.

Once, during this period of the late 1970's, I spoke to the local district judge, Ronald Jones, in Ada, about trying to get some help for Ronnie, but Judge Jones informed me that the courts could do nothing about Ronnie until it could be proven that he was either a danger to himself or others."

Gary Simmons and Renee Williamson, Ron Williamson's youngest sister, were married in 1971, the same year Ron transferred to Asher, Oklahoma, for his senior year in high school.

"After Ron was drafted by the Oakland A's, Renee and I were aware that Ron's dad had received several phone calls from his coach," Gary said. "The coach was concerned with Ron's behavior. Apparently Ron was complaining to the coach about not getting enough playing time and was generally difficult to get along with.

Finally, when Ron's arm began to give him trouble and he was cut from the team, Ron was devastated. He knew the sacrifices his family had made for him throughout the years so that he could focus on baseball and he felt like he had let them down. He felt like a terrible failure. This was when his emotional problems really began to surface. He worked in Tulsa, Oklahoma as a promotional representative with Southwestern Bell Telephone Company, but it wasn't a job he liked or was very good at.

I remember once, before Ron and Patty were divorced, Renee and I went to a wedding in Tulsa and we stayed with them. Ron seemed very nervous and agitated. He paced around the house continuously for some time and then he just left without saying a word to any of us. Patty was very upset and told us that he had done that on other occasions. There was another time when Ron and Patty came to visit with us. Ron and I went to see a movie. The only thing

Ron could talk about the entire weekend was this movie and he was upset that no one else wanted to talk about it.

I have never seen anyone with such an obsessive personality. He could have only one focus at a time and he became so totally immersed in whatever that was that he excluded everything else in his life. Once he became focused on American Presidents and for weeks that was all he talked about.

Renee and I moved away from Ada after Ron and Patty were divorced, but when we would come back there for family gatherings, holidays and such, Ron would do two things I thought were very strange. He would stay in a room by himself with the door closed, and then he would come out shouting, ranting and raving about something totally different from what we were all doing at the time. For instance, there was one Christmas when Ronnie burst into the room where the rest of us had been enjoying each other's company. He sat on the floor and started playing a guitar. He demanded that we all sing. Suddenly, he got up and went to his room and closed the door. We just looked at each other and rolled our eyes.

I remember when he had job at a men's clothing store in Ada. He became obsessed with fashion. He was a handsome guy and he seemed to like good clothes, but he would constantly tell everyone how to dress, which tie was right and which was wrong. The job there didn't last long either.

There was another strange incident at our house in Chickasha, Oklahoma. Several family members were sitting in the living room engaged in conversation when Ron went into the bathroom. When he came out he began shouting and rambling about religion. He was insensate about it and nothing he said made any sense at all. This may have been the only way he could get any attention, but it was weird and it was getting worse.

The next day after the family left, Ron disappeared. His behavior had become so strange that we were at a loss to know what to do. One Sunday Renee and I had gone to church and when we came back, Ron came around to the front of the house. He had been sleeping out behind our back yard fence he told us, because he had been in Lawton, Oklahoma, at Ft Sill where he had escaped from some Army guys where they had guns and explosives in their homes and were planning to overthrow the base.

He wanted to stay with us and I let him have my son's room. He got a job hauling hay for a local farmer. The job lasted two days.

Ron told me he had found a softball team to play on, but a few days later the man who organized the team called and told me Ron wasn't welcome because he had too many emotional problems.

Ron was basically nocturnal at this point. He wouldn't or couldn't sleep at night. He would stay up all night in the living room with the television on, and then he would go to bed when the sun began to come up. He complained of headaches often.

His eating habits became strange. He ate like a voracious animal with an insatiable appetite. It was almost like he was afraid he would never get another meal.

Finally, I told him that if he was going to stay with us he had to follow the same program the rest of my family had. He had to get up in the morning and sleep at night. Ron didn't seem to recognize that he had any problems at all. He told me that he might have some medical problems, like mono or encephalitis, and that it affected his appetite and his sleeping habits. Eventually, his behavior was seriously beginning to affect my family and I had to tell him to leave. He went back to Ada and lived with his mother.

In 1985, Ron was arrested for illegally obtaining three hundred dollars from East Central University in Ada. The police put him under house arrest, and then put him in jail for not being home when they came to check on him. This was about a week before his mother died. I had to go to the jail to prepare him for his mother's dying.

The jailers wouldn't let either of his sisters go back to his cell to see him. I looked through the small opening in the door of his cell. Ron was standing nude with his back to the door. I called to him three times and did not get a response. Then, suddenly he turned around and started shouting at me. He was very abusive and threatened to kick my ass. This was way out of character for Ron as he had always had respect for me in the past. The jailer made me leave.

I have taken Ron to Central State Hospital on at least two occasions, and I arranged for him to be accepted into the 'teen challenge program' with the help of our local minister. It was a program designed for ex-cons, alcoholics and drug addicts. The program was church oriented. I talked with our pastor and he agreed to get Ron admitted. The pastor's real observation was that Ron had problems that the program couldn't help him with. The pastor's comment was: "Ron's lights are on, but nobody's home". We were desperate, so we made the appointment to go to Dallas and let him be entered into the program there anyway. Ron was taking lithium at this time; however, because the church sponsors the program, they did not allow anyone to have medications, cigarettes, alcohol and unknown to me, they did not let any of the participants have any money. After he was checked in, I gave Ron fifty dollars in case there was anything he needed. Ronnie bought a bus ticket that afternoon and was back in Ada the next day.

The last time I took Ron to Central State Hospital was a real nightmare. I had two of my friends over to watch a ball game when the doorbell rang. It was Ron. He came in and said, "I need help." He collapsed on my living room floor. He was unshaven and his hair was matted and unkempt. His clothes were dirty and wrinkled. He was very disoriented. "I need help – I'm crazy. I just can't take it anymore."

At first he appeared to be agitated and fidgety, then he became lethargic and almost catatonic. I told him to hang on and we would get him some help. One of my friends went with me and we drove him to the Grady County Memorial Hospital. They referred us to Grady County Health Department, who in turn told us to take him to Central State Hospital in Norman and check him in.

On the way to Norman, Ron told me he was hungry and needed something to eat. I drove him to a barbeque place and as we drove into the parking lot, Ron looked at me asked where we were. I told him we were going to get him something to eat and he said that he wasn't hungry, so we went on. He seemed terribly frustrated and fifteen minutes later told me he was starving. We stopped at a McDonalds on the turnpike and he again refused to eat. He said he just wanted to get to the hospital. As we drove into Norman, I stopped for gas and then bought a couple of candy bars that I gave to Ron and he devoured them in a matter of seconds.

At the hospital, a doctor came into the emergency room to see Ron. Ron was drifting in and out and the doctor couldn't get him to cooperate. It was like Ron was a small child who was scared. After the doctor left the room Ron went over and faced a blank wall. He assumed a body-builder like pose. He stood, rigid and looked at the ceiling, not moving a muscle or making a sound. He stood that way for over half an hour. I attempted to talk to him but I got no response at all. Eventually some of the staff came and took him to a room. Ron checked himself out, against the advice of the hospital, the next day. They couldn't keep him against his will because he had checked himself in voluntarily.

This kind of behavior had gone on for about ten years. No matter what avenue we tried, we couldn't get Ron institutionalized long enough for him to get effective help."

Renee added other strange behavior patterns after the Carter murder. "During part of the time after the murder, Ron would arrive at a family gathering and become extremely nervous. He would shake all over and then leave the room. The most obvious thing was the change in his physical appearance. He had always been particular about his clothes and grooming, but during this time he became increasingly sloppy and unkempt. He refused to eat with the family and would eat long after everyone else had finished

I remember once when the family was visiting another relative near Tulsa. Ron was a houseguest at the time. During the night, the relative caught Ron getting some liquor out of the cabinet. He took the bottle away from him and poured it down the sink. There was such a commotion that the entire household was aroused. Ron stood in the middle of the living room and began to ramble about his life and how terrible it was. He talked for more than an hour without interruption. It was," she said, "as if we were not there. The relative tried to calm him down but he talked even faster and waved his arms for emphasis. Finally, he slumped into a chair totally exhausted.

Another time, when he was incarcerated in the County Jail in Ada on the bogus check charge, he became fascinated with the Bible. My sister, Annette, and I had come to visit him and he spoke to us as if we were strangers. He invited us to step right up, acting as if he were some kind of radio broadcaster. He began to tell Bible stories and paid no attention to us. We let him talk until he finally stopped. It was strange because he suddenly became rational and we carried on a normal conversation with him as if nothing had happened.

After Ron moved back to Ada and lived with our mother," Renee said, "she told me that he claimed that he was hearing voices that told him he was bad and would never be any better. He told her that the Lord had told him to pray and ask for help to clear his mind."

"I was never asked by Ron's attorney to testify at Ron's trial for the murder of Debbie Carter, and neither Renee nor Annette were asked to testify," Gary Simmons said. "We didn't know that we could testify. Had we been ask to testify about the mental condition of Ron Williamson we would have been happy to do so."

CHAPTER SEVEN

The morning of December 9, 1982, Dennis Fritz called the high school in Noble Oklahoma, where he taught math and science, to say that he was sick. The school arranged for a substitute teacher for the day.

Noble, a small community, some forty miles northwest of Ada had a population of less than one thousand residents, so housing was limited. Dennis had lived in Ada for some time. He taught at another small school in Konawa, Oklahoma, before he accepted the job in Noble. Dennis was a single father. His daughter, Elizabeth was eight years old. Dennis's mother had moved from her home in Kansas City, Missouri to Ada to help Dennis care for Elizabeth after the death of Dennis's wife in 1975. Dennis felt comfortable with Elizabeth's school in Ada and his mother liked the town. Dennis had established friendships in Ada and the drive to the school where he taught was an easy one. Dennis rented a house less than three blocks from Marie Simpson's rental properties.

Dennis spent his high school years in Talihina, Oklahoma, a small eastern Oklahoma community located in the Kiamichi Mountains. These mountains are known for the deep, clear lakes and the lush foliage of pine trees, oaks and dogwood. The tourists appear in the spring to view the white dogwood and the deep pink redwood blossoms. In the fall when the leaves turn red and orange this precarious road, named the Talihimina Drive, through the mountains is crowded with cars. The nearest town to Talihina is Wilburton and has a population of over three thousand people. Wilburton was the home of the Dalton Brothers and the famous outlaw, Belle Starr. The Talihimina Drive received its name from Queen Wilhimina of the Netherlands who once visited there. A lodge named for her stands at the crest of this mountain overlooking the canyons below.

Dennis's father disappeared early in his life and his mother worked various restaurant jobs in the area. Dennis was devoted to her, a still young, attractive woman, who continued to have hopes of finding a stable relationship with a man who would take care of both Dennis and herself.

Dennis was a popular student in this mountain community. He was good looking and athletic, participating in all the sports activities. The girls liked him. He was never without a date for any of the school activities. He had dark hair and sharp blue eyes and although he was less than six feet tall, he was a great runner and a track star. The football coach suspected, early on, that Dennis would be a great addition to his football team that year, and he was right. Dennis became an outstanding member of the team his senior year and the team won the state championship in their class.

    Not only was he a good athlete, he was an excellent student. His high school teacher, Sandra Mantooth, said that he wrote the best essay she had ever read. In her high school yearbook, Dennis wrote: "To Miss Mantooth, a real cool teacher who I like a lot. It's been lots of fun having class with you this year. Fritz."

    After graduation, Dennis enrolled at Southeastern State University in Durant, Oklahoma. One of the students who had been in his graduating class, Mary Smith, whose mother was the home economics teacher there, was standing in the same line to enroll. Dennis and Mary had not dated in high school, but the attraction was obvious. Mary was a beautiful, blonde girl and Dennis was smitten. They were a handsome couple and they married over the Christmas holidays in their freshman year. Both were bright and optimistic, with plans for further education and the promise of a good life.

    Dennis's athletic scholarship to Southeastern, and his part time job provided enough income to support them, even after the birth of their daughter, Elizabeth in 1971, but Mary decided to postpone her education until Elizabeth was in school. The rent on the mobile home where they lived was cheap and they needed only one car which was second hand and inexpensive to operate.

    The winter of 1975 was unseasonably cold. On Christmas Eve, several inches of snow fell during the afternoon while Dennis was studying in the library. The clouds were heavy with the promise of more of the white stuff as Dennis loaded his books into the back seat of the car and drove to the trailer park. He stopped at a convenience store near the campus and picked up milk and some candy for Elizabeth's Christmas stocking. Then he saw a stuffed bear with a red ribbon around its neck. Elizabeth loved bears. The toys had been reduced to half price. Dennis bought the bear and put it into the bag with the milk and candy.

    As he drove the car under the makeshift carport by the trailer, he noticed that there were no lights on in the house. It was past five o'clock and the low hanging clouds made it appear much later. The air was still. The only noise was the crunching sound his shoes made as he walked through the fallen snow.

The door to the trailer was unlocked and slightly ajar. He heard a soft whimpering sound coming from Elizabeth's bedroom. He turned on the living room light and rushed to open Elizabeth's door. She was sitting on the floor hugging her favorite doll. He picked her up and she buried her head under his chin as she hugged to doll even closer to her chest. Without turning on the light in the room he and Mary shared, he pushed the door open. Elizabeth's back was toward the bed where Mary lay. Mary was very still. He backed away and closed the door. He didn't want Elizabeth to see. She was only four years old.

When the police arrived, Dennis was sitting on the front step of the trailer. He and Elizabeth were wrapped in a blanket from her bed watching the snow fall in big flakes as she tried to catch them with her chubby fingers.

There had been rumors of a child molester in the neighborhood. This man had attempted to abduct children in the area, but no one had been able to give a description of him. He was clever, the police said. Mary must have put up quite a struggle to protect her child, they added. She had been shot in the head, they told Dennis. Several times, they added.

Months later, a man was arrested and charged with this crime.

When the school in Noble discovered that Dennis Fritz was on the suspect list in the murder of Debbie Carter, they terminated his contract. Dennis, along with a dozen other men who had been customers at the Coachlight were required to give fingerprints, blood and saliva samples to the police.

The breakfast crowd at the Parkview Café had a number of opinions regarding the murder.

"Heard Ron Williamson's on the top of the suspect list in that Carter girl's murder," the old man said to his younger friend.

"Nobody's surprised about that. Ron's documented crazy. Lots of women in this town are scared to death of him."

"That other fella, that Fritz guy – the teacher," the old man said, "I hear he'd kind of taken up with Ron."

"Both of 'em single and all - Ron divorced and Fritz a widower. Still it seems like a strange mix to me."

"What happened to Fritz's wife?"

"Murdered – over there in Durant at the college."

"Good, lord."

" The police report says that girl's apartment was wrecked. They think there had to be two people who killed her."

"Who told you that?"

"I'm not at liberty to say."

After the breakfast crowd cleared out, Agnes said to the cook, "How come they don't just arrest that Ron and Dennis – seems to me they're real mean guys."

"Good lord, Agnes," the cook said. "It ain't legal to arrest somebody on circumstantial evidence."

"What's that mean?"

"Circumstantial means they don't have any proof."

"Well, anyway, they seem to be guilty as sin."

"That's what I'm telling you."

"What?"

"What you see ain't always what's the truth."

"I'm not ignorant," Agnes said. "I can understand that."

CHAPTER EIGHT

In April of 1983, when the jonquils were in bloom and the dogwood trees heavy with the first blossoms of the season, the winter night of December 8, 1982, and the tragedy of Debbie Carter was overshadowed by the disappearance and possible murder of another young woman.

Patty Hamilton, an eighteen-year-old woman was abducted from a convenience store in Seminole, Oklahoma, some thirty miles from Ada, but in the same judicial district. This became an unsolved case that plagued OSBI agent Gary Rogers and Detective Smith. She was reported missing on the morning of April 10, 1983, her car locked, her purse inside the car and her car keys on the counter by the cash register. Money was missing from the store. Every piece of evidence led to a dead end. She had not been heard from or seen since that night. Without a body there is no case.

One year later, in April of 1984, Denise Haraway, a student at East Central University in Ada, was abducted from her part time job at a convenience store. She was the wife of another student, Steve Haraway, whose father was a prominent dentist in town. There were witnesses who reported seeing her leave with two men, however, money was taken from the cash register and her purse and car keys were left on the counter. Her disappearance, sixteen months after the Carter murder, left the residents of this community fearful and demanding action by the police and the authorities.

Dennis Smith, the detective who had been the first on the scene of the Carter murder, was seething. He grew up in the same neighborhood where the Carter family lived and remembered Debbie as a toddler. The lack of any evidence linking any one of the suspects to this crime left him helpless. He had looked at the photographs at the Carter crime scene dozens of times. They made him sick to his stomach.

The anonymous calls from irate citizens flooded the police department and the district attorney's office. They threatened to find and punish whoever was responsible for both the Carter murder, the Hamilton disappearance and now the mystery surrounding the Haraway abduction, reminding the authorities that the pecan tree in the court house yard would be a proper place for a hanging in all three of these cases.

The district attorney, Bill Peterson, and the law enforcement officers didn't need three unsolved murders in two years on their books.

Detective Smith, a veteran of over sixteen years with the police department, made his own rules. Barrel-chested, short and bald, he preferred wearing golf shirts even when a coat and tie might have been a better choice. When questioning a prisoner, his voice could turn harsh without warning, and his sense of humor was more sadistic than funny. Some said that his pale blue eyes held a threatening glint. "Watch out for them eyes," more than one criminal he helped put behind bars would say.

Smith and his wife, Sandi, lived in a rambling style house seven miles south of town. This comfortable home with its redwood deck and swimming pool was surrounded by two acres of lawn and tall oak trees. He and Sandi, who worked as a building inspector for the city of Ada, supported this above average lifestyle with numerous part time jobs. One had been a paper route where Detective Smith drove the car as Sandi tossed six hundred and fifty copies of The Daily Oklahoman onto the lawns of the subscribers. Lifestyle was important in Ada, and no one understood this better than Dennis Smith.

He was born in Ada in 1943. His grandfather was one of the early settlers, who moved there from Arkansas before statehood and became a great friend of Jeff Reed, the principal founder of Ada.

As a toddler, during those post war years, Dennis played in the quiet neighborhoods of this sleepy town where doors were seldom locked and the residents feared God, but never their neighbors.

When he was in third grade, he went to a charity camp called Sheep Creek. Sheep Creek is located ten miles outside the city in a beautiful, secluded area with hiking trails. Shadowed by the tall oaks and pines, a spacious lodge and Olympic sized pool are nestled into this natural setting. The clear mountain lake, which borders this property, is perfect for fishing and swimming. Lifesaving equipment was not commonly available in those years, but in a concern for safety, gallon cans were strapped to the boy's chests when they learned to swim.

The wealthy Norris family owned this property and generously provided the use of it for groups sponsoring youth activities and other civic meetings.

In Junior High School, Smith met a boy named Bill Peterson. Bill's grandfather, P.A. Norris, owned not only Sheep Creek, but more than a thousand acres of oil producing land in Pontotoc County. He also owned the First National Bank where Dennis's father worked sweeping floors.

Ada, like many small communities in Oklahoma, knew few boundaries when it came to rich and poor. Dennis and Bill played sports together and hung around in the same crowd. Most families were employed, living in modest homes and paying their bills in the prosperity of the 1950's. When Dennis, along with other boys his age, was invited to the Peterson home, it seemed like a palace when compared to his own modest home.

This friendship between Smith and Peterson continued through most of high school. When Smith graduated from Ada High School, he enlisted in the Marines. He was stationed in California, between the Korean and Vietnam conflicts, and even considered a military career. The benefits were good and he respected the discipline, but he missed the small town atmosphere of Ada. It was home, and the opportunity for further education was available for him at East Central University.

After completing his bachelor's degree, he joined the police force where he spent nine years as a uniformed officer. It was a good job and he was good at the job. The benefits were excellent and after twenty years, he could retire at half the pay of his highest salary.

Bill Peterson, after his graduation from Ada High, also went into the military service, but staying in any branch of the military after his time was fulfilled never occurred to him. He enrolled in Southwestern University in Weatherford, Oklahoma, and graduated with a BA in business administration. It was here that he met and married his wife, Dean, and decided to enroll in law school at Oklahoma City University.

One of his classmates was Greg Saunders.

Saunders, too, had ties to Ada. His maternal grandparents lived in the community of Francis, a town about ten miles north of Ada. He visited these grandparents during summer vacations and holidays. After his graduation from high school in Virginia, he enrolled at East Central University, but his undergraduate days were interrupted by the Vietnam war. He became an officer in the U. S. Marine Corps and his time there was spent flying jets in this conflict.

Saunders was a weight lifter, broad shouldered and sturdy. He had a brilliant smile and a full head of salt and pepper shaded hair. By the time of the 1988 trial, he had a successful law practice in the worker's comp field, an ex wife, two teen age children and a new wife who was also a lawyer practicing in Ada. Peterson and Saunders graduated from law school in 1975 and were admitted to the bar that same year.

Peterson was the only child of Marjorie Norris Peterson who had married William A. Peterson, a medical doctor several years her senior. Dr. Peterson, also a member of one of Ada's prominent families, was well known for his eccentricities. For fifty years he practiced medicine in a small office behind the pharmacy that filled every prescription he ever wrote. The citizens could set their watches by his comings and goings. He arrived promptly at eight o'clock every morning and left at five p.m.

Although the Peterson family could never compete with the Norris family monetarily, it was grounded in academic achievement and those two attributes balanced the scales of social acceptance nicely. But, the events, which bound them together more securely, were those of disaster.

The Norris family was tragically star crossed. P. A. Norris had three sons and two daughters, Marjorie and Susan. While in their teens, two of his sons were killed when the car they were riding in was hit by a train. The other son was later killed in a plane crash. The elder Norris, despite the loss of his three sons, felt some solace in the knowledge that his two daughters married into financially and socially acceptable families with professional backgrounds.

Dr. Peterson was forty years old when Bill was born. Bill was an agreeable youngster, good looking with dark hair and brown eyes. Although not particularly inspired to excel in academics or sports, he participated in both and became a popular student both with his peers and his teachers. Of course, the need to excel was not the compelling goal in his life as he already lived in one of the largest homes on Kings Row, and in Ada, that was a goal in and of itself.

At the age of seventy-two, Dr. Peterson decided to cut down a tree on his property. He left his office promptly at five o'clock, drove to his home, changed clothes and got his chain saw out of his barn. He had talked about cutting down the tree for sometime and had been warned by Bill, as well as his wife, not to do it by himself. Dr. Peterson, however, never took advice from anyone.

After his wife returned home from her weekly bridge game at the Country Club, she suspected that something was wrong. The garage door was open with the doctor's car parked inside. He never failed to close the garage door. His wife called Bill at his office. Remembering the tree, Bill immediately drove to the spot where the troublesome tree grew. His father lay beneath the tree. It was obvious from the position of his body that he had seen the tree falling and tried to scramble out of its way, but tripped on some weeds that were wrapped around his ankles.

After Bill Peterson graduated from law school, he and Dean moved back to Ada. The practice of law didn't interest him much, but he became very interested in politics. The district attorney's job was open and he decided to run for the office. He had the personality of a good politician. Plus, he was handsome, friendly and eager to please which were characteristics that made him a favorite with the voters and he won handily. These voters, of course, knew his background and he seemed less likely to be dishonest since he was financially secure.

Life was good in Ada. The low crime rate and the stable population made it a fine place to raise a family. Children could walk to school without fear. The teachers kept in close touch with the parents of their students. The sports programs in the school system were excellent. With the exception of the cement plant, which employed a large number of the citizens, there was little industry and industry was not encouraged. The shops were independently owned, even the grocery stores still delivered to the homes of their customers. The "flower" children of the sixties were slow to find Ada. They belonged to the "beatnik generation" in San Francisco and Los Angeles. But, by the late sixties and early seventies, marijuana infiltrated the college and high school crowd. Some of the parents were outraged that drugs were being traded in the community while others accepted it as a rite of passage. Alcohol had always been the drug of choice with the adults, and they reasoned that smoking a little weed wasn't as dangerous as alcohol.

When the oil boom in the late seventies brought Oklahoma's economy the largest boost since the one during the depression years of the thirties, the men in the states not blessed with jobs from both the east and west coasts migrated to Oklahoma. With them came, not only marijuana and other drugs, heroin, cocaine and something called Quaaludes, but it brought the money to buy them.

CHAPTER NINE

From October 1, 1984 to January 23, 1985, Ron Williamson was in the county jail in Ada on bogus check charges. During this stay, a woman who went by the name of Terri Holland was also in the county jail. She had three felony convictions, one being a federal conviction for conspiracy to defraud the federal government, another for forgery and the last for passing bogus checks in Pontotoc County where Ada is the county seat.

This incarceration was not Terri Holland's first stay in the jail in Ada. She was a frequent inmate, young, blonde and attractive in a kind of used up way. She happened to be a good listener and the police used her to talk and listen to certain prisoners. She usually wore shorts and a long tee shirt. Tiny blue and yellow flowers were tattooed from her ankles up her thighs.

She said that she heard Ron Williamson's confession that he had a dream that he killed Debra Carter. The eight hundred dollar check charge against her was ultimately reduced to three hundred dollars and her sentence, in spite of the fact that she had two other felony charges, was suspended to less than eighteen months. She would be an important witness for the prosecution in the 1988 trial.

During Ron Williamson's incarceration in the county jail in the winter of 1984, several mental health practitioners examined him. In spite of the lengthy history of mental illness, including schizophrenia, bipolar disorder, borderline personality disorder and paranoid personality disorder which dated back to 1979, and an actual determination of his incompetence in the same district court in an unrelated case, the competency of Williamson to stand trial was never determined.

Actually, on September 25, 1985, a special district judge for the District Court of Pontotoc County, found Williamson mentally ill and unable to assist counsel. He had been charged with escape from house arrest for a bogus check conviction. The judge in that case officially adjudged and decreed that Williamson was unable to appreciate the nature of the charges against him, consult with his attorney or rationally assist in his defense. This court found that, "He is a mentally ill person who requires treatment as defined by Oklahoma statutes. The court based its findings on an evaluation by

Dr. Charles W. Amos who indicated that Williamson was "delusional" and recommended transfer to Eastern State Hospital for evaluation. From September 30, 1985 to October 30, 1985, he was under observation there.

Dr. R.D. Garcia, in his written opinion stated that Williamson was competent, but prescribed, Thorazine, Dalmanne, Ristoril, Duedcin and Merraril. The Thorazine dosage he recommended was 100 mg four times a day. Dr. Garcia also found Williamson to be a sociopath. Dr. Garcia was employed by the State of Oklahoma in all competency evaluations.

In a letter from Ms Norma Walker, a social worker with Mental Health Services of Southern Okalahoma, outlined the information contained in Williamson's chart with that institution, including the various times he utilized the services of that facility since 1980, wrote: "This client has been suspected by some counselors of shamming and malingering to manipulate the system. My belief is that he needs a complete neurological evaluation by professionals as an inpatient. This is the only way to obtain a differential diagnosis in the case."

No neuropsychological evaluation was made.

Another letter from Ms Walker on February 20, 1987, stated: "I last saw Ron Williamson on February 20, 1987, and he was not capable of managing his daily living activities. He was greatly impaired in his ability to make reasonable life decisions. He was disoriented as to time and impaired in his attention span. At times he became delusional, showing an associational disturbance and confused thinking. He was unable to take care of his own needs for food or shelter. He was unmedicated at that time and refused to take medication. His perceptions of reality were seriously distorted. He would be unable to care for himself without being medicated and would be hard to manage, even with medication. I expect him to need long term institutionalization for his diminished mental capacities and unmanageable behavior."

Williamson was awarded Social Security Disability benefits because of his mental illness, on November 9, 1987. The Administrative Law Judge made the following findings regarding the Social Security Disability award to Williamson: "There are repeated episodes of disorientation to time, impaired attention span, as well as impaired abstract thinking and level of consciousness. He is delusional, also showing an associational disturbance and confused thinking. It's not possible to tell when the claimant became sufficiently impaired as to be classified as disabled because of his mental impairments, but the evidence of record would indicate that it did occur on or prior to the time that the claimant last met the listings on March 31, 1985."

CHAPTER TEN

In April of 1987, many of the residents of Ada had forgotten about the night of December 8, 1982, and the tragic death of Debbie Carter. There had been no news concerning this crime. No arrests had been made and little or no information disclosed.

One of the reasons for the lack of evidence at the crime scene stemmed form the fact that the criminalist for the OSBI, Mary Long, said that the body fluids collected from Carter's body and other evidence collected from the apartment indicated that the assailants or assailant were non-secretors. "A non-secretor," she stated, "is a person who does not secrete blood in their bodily fluids. As a result, the blood type of the attacker or attackers could not be determined by simple blood tests." From her tests, she concluded that both Fritz and Williamson were non-secretors. She also believed that Debbie Carter was a non-secretor. Long admitted that as many as eleven of the nineteen suspects who were present at the Coachlight on that December night who gave saliva samples could have been non-secretors; however, she admitted that not all of those nineteen suspects were given blood tests of any kind. Also, none of the fingerprints in the Carter apartment were ever identified as belonging to any one of the interviewed suspects, including Dennis Fritz and Ron Williamson.

The only piece of evidence that had not been inspected was the piece of wall in Debbie Carter's apartment, which contained the bloody palm print.

The evidence was located at the crime lab in Oklahoma City, carefully preserved in brown paper to protect blood evidence. The reason a final judgment had never been made as to the identity of this print was because of the condition of the deceased. Her hands were clinched and the medical examiner was unable to loosen them enough for an examination.

To exhume a body requires a great deal of preparation. It must be done without notice to the public. Complicated orders and releases from the family are required and the actual grave opening is usually done during nighttime hours to create as little curiosity as possible.

Bill Peterson wanted this case to come to trial and be over with once and for all. The members of his staff, along with the photographer and the assistant medical examiner were there when Debbie Carter's casket was opened.

The day had been cool and damp and rain had fallen during the afternoon. A backhoe scooped away the topsoil from the grave and a forklift tractor eased its steel fingers underneath the coffin and lifted it to the surface. The coffin was brushed free of dirt and the six clasps snapped open. The medical examiner opened the top half of the lid and swung it back.

It had been five years since her death. No one knew what changes time might have made on the body of this young woman. Old wives tales told horror stories of black mold covering the faces of the corpse, hair that fell away after time, but when the lights flashed over her, it was as if time had stood still. Her face was clear, her hair full. It could have been only yesterday that the funeral was held. The local medical examiner unclasped her fingers and made the prints as the group gathered there watched. The prints were placed in protective covering and would be sent to the State Medical Examiner's office that night.

Keeping a secret in a small town is difficult. Floyd Jones*, an indigent person in Ada, lived in a shack near the railroad tracks and picked up cans and glass bottles along the highway and the tracks. He rode a discarded bicycle that he had found at the trash dump near his residence. This means of transportation was all he needed to support his lifestyle. In spite of his long hair, beard and generally unkempt appearance, Floyd was harmless.

Floyd was a nocturnal person. After the local restaurants closed and the grocery store clerks had gone home, he visited the trash bins located behind these establishments. He was a discerning shopper. There were usually some overripe bananas, a loaf or two of day old bread and occasionally a cake or pie to be found at the end of the day. The Parkview Café was another dependable source. Agnes often left food for Floyd by the back door. She knew that he was mildly retarded and she understood poverty in a personal way.

The morning after Debbie Carter's body was exhumed, Agnes saw Floyd rummaging through the trash bin behind the café. She took half an apple pie that had been in the pie case on the counter and put it on a paper plate. She opened the back door, motioned to Floyd and handed him the pie.

"There's been a grave robbing out to the Rosedale Cemetery," he whispered to her.

"How'd you know that?"

"I seen it."

"When?"

"Last night."

"What you doing out there at that grave yard in the night?"

"I was just a riding by. It's usually mighty quiet out there most times."

"Who was it?"

"Don't know. There was more than one. Lights too."

He put the pie into the basket attached to the handle-bars.

"That don't seem right." Agnes frowned.

"Much obliged for the pie," Floyd said as he rode away.

Later in the day, one of the Sheriff's deputies came into the café and sat at the counter. Agnes poured coffee for him and leaned against the counter, arms folded across her chest.

"Heard there was a grave robbing out to the Rosedale Cemetery last night."

"It ain't no big deal," the deputy said, stirring sugar into his cup. "I've seen 'em do it before – once."

"Digging up a dead body ain't no big deal?"

"Not when it's about evidence in a murder case," he said.

"A murder case," she repeated. "I'll bet it was that Carter girl."

"You didn't hear it from me," he said.

"I won't tell a soul."

"Well, hell, Agnes, it's been five years since she got killed. The folks around here want to have somebody arrested."

"Then who's gonna be arrested?"

"I can't rightly say. Can I have one of those chocolate donuts?"

"It's on the house," she said as she reached for the plate and put it in front of him.

On May 7, 1987, the official report from the crime lab in Oklahoma City arrived in Ada. The identification of the palm print was entered into evidence. The print was that of the deceased.

"Are we ready to roll?" Detective Smith asked Gary Rogers, the

OSBI agent.

"Let's go over the evidence we've got," Rogers said. "There's no third suspect. We've got Terri Holland's story about the dream, the non-secretor report from Mary Long, and the hair comparison report."

"Now, let's go over the evidence we don't have," Smith said. "We don't have any fingerprints, we don't have any witnesses that remember either Williamson or Fritz being at the Coachlight that night."

"Let's back up now," Rogers interrupted. "We've got James Harjo and Mike Tenney."

"Harjo's completely incompetent and a snitch, just like Terri Holland, and Tenney's a suck up trying to get on the force."

"We've got somebody else that you may have forgotten about," Rogers said. "Remember Glen Gore? He was at the club that night and he said he saw Williamson bothering Carter."

"Well, yeah, but he's in jail. On a kidnapping, rape and shooting with intent charge. Who's gonna believe him?"

"It's worth a try."

CHAPTER ELEVEN

Ada high school football is legendary in the State of Oklahoma. The win record of the team gives the community a great deal of recognition, not only state wide, but many of the players are recruited nationally. Record crowds are in attendance at the Friday night games held at Norris Field, which is the stadium for East Central University.

Glen Gore could have been one of those sought after members of the Ada team. When he was in junior high school, he became the boy to watch and the high school coaches were looking forward to having him on the field. He loved the game and he was fast and well coordinated. One of his junior high teachers remembered him as a quiet boy. He expressed little interest in academic achievement, but seemed to be simply marking time in the classroom until he could be on the playing field, she said.

Of Indian parentage, he was good looking with swarthy skin, thick black hair and a wide smile that attracted girls. He ran to keep in shape for sports, worked at hard jobs that required physical effort and often worked hauling hay for the farmers in the area.

The summer before his sophomore year, he began working out with the team. The coaches watched his performance and were looking forward to having him on the starting team in the fall. However, soon after school began, he was arrested for drug possession. The charge, because it was a first offence, was reduced to a misdemeanor, but after the second arrest which involved drugs and alcohol, he was dismissed from school, and, of course, the football team. Arrangements were made for him to continue his education at another high school in the district, but no record exists of Glen Gore in the alternate school.

When he was sober, he was quiet and well behaved, but when he had too much to drink, his personality changed. Because he was strong and muscular, he soon discovered he had the ability to win a fight by simple brute force.

In 1984, Gore married a girl whose father managed a shoe store in Ada, and he became the father of a beautiful baby girl. The marriage was short lived, as his bouts with drugs and alcohol became too much for his wife and she filed for divorce.

On the front page of the Ada Evening News dated January 1, 1988, the headline read: ARRESTS LEAD THE LIST OF THE TOP TEN STORIES OF 1987. At the top of the list was the arrest of Ron Williamson and Dennis Fritz for the murder of Debbie Carter. Seventh on the list was the arrest of Glen Gore who had held his ex wife and his two year old daughter hostage at gunpoint in her home for several hours before releasing them and surrendering to the police. He was sentenced to one hundred and sixty years, four forty year sentences, those being first degree burglary, kidnapping, shooting with intent to kill and feloniously pointing a weapon.

After Gore was in prison in the State Penitentiary at McAlester, Oklahoma, a letter was received by the district court in Ada from the parents of the woman who was held hostage by him. The letter stated: "We want you to be aware of how dangerous we feel this man is. He intends to kill our daughter, our granddaughter and ourselves. This he has told us. We have gone to great lengths to make our daughter's home burglar proof, but all has failed. To go into detail of all the times he has attacked her would make too lengthy a letter. Please give our daughter enough time to get the child raised before he is out of prison and the terror starts again."

One week after Gore was listed as an additional witness in the Williamson and Fritz cases, a plea bargain agreement was entered and a second kidnapping charge and a charge of assault and battery with a dangerous weapon were then dropped.

The letter from the terrified parents of the young woman and her daughter was filed on June 3, 1987, and disappeared in Gore's criminal file.

Although hair samples from Gore were taken in 1982, as they were from the other men on the suspect list, the forensic experts never examined them and the OSBI failed to compare them to the other unidentified hairs found in the Carter apartment. Rather, the State's expert inexplicably compared the Gore hairs to the slides he was preparing to testify about in court, i.e., the hairs he had already identified as microscopically consistent with Debra Carter, Williamson and Fritz. Although fingerprints for twenty-three suspects and twenty-one other individuals who had been in the victim's apartment were sent to the OSBI for comparison with the prints found in the victim's apartment, Gore's fingerprints were never submitted.

CHAPTER TWELVE

On May 8, 1987, felony murder charges were filed against Ron Williamson and Dennis Fritz in the death of Debra Carter. It was a mild weather day, with sunshine and a few puffy, white clouds dotting the sky. Ron Williamson had oiled the old lawnmower and was trying it out on his mother's yard first. About the only work he could get was yard work and he was meticulous about it, edging the driveways just so and carefully bagging the grass. It was the beginning of summer yard work and he was looking forward to being outdoors.

He saw the police car slowing down in front of the house before it turned into the drive. He walked toward the car, smiling, intending to ask them if they were looking for something, when Dennis Smith and Gary Rogers got out of the car, guns drawn and told him to "hit it!" They pinned him to the ground and cuffed him without saying a word.

Dennis Fritz began working construction jobs in Ada after his teaching job was terminated. His mother and his daughter, Elizabeth moved back to Kansas City, Missouri, because of the publicity of the Carter murder and after a few months, he moved there as well. He picked up odd jobs and was trying to plan a future. Nothing had happened in the Carter murder case and he assumed that his name was cleared.

He had been painting his mother's house on May 8, 1987, and about 10:00p.m., he stretched out on the on the living room couch and was watching the late news when the doorbell rang. He looked through the window toward the driveway and saw a police car. When he opened the door, Gary Rogers and Dennis Smith grabbed him and cuffed his hands behind his back. He was shoved into the police car and driven back to Ada that night and placed in the Pontotoc County jail.

In 1987 there was no public defender in Pontotoc County. Each member of the county bar association was required to take a turn representing indigent defendants. The attorney appointed by the presiding judge, received compensation, however, the pay of $3,500.00, was fixed, whether the trial and the preparation took one week or one year. The State provided funds for expert witnesses and research, but indigent defendants had no such resources. Most attorneys did not relish a court appointment and particularly when it involved a high profile trial.

Ronald Jones, the presiding judge, appointed the two attorneys who were next on the appointment list. Barney Ward, who had been practicing in Ada for more than forty years, was appointed to defend Ron Williamson. Ward had been blind since he was involved in a chemistry class accident when he was in high school. In spite of this handicap, he maintained a successful law practice and in his younger years, had been a prosecutor, but now he was at an age where he was looking forward to retirement. Judge Jones also appointed Greg Saunders to defend Dennis Fritz.

This should have been an easy case for the defense. Neither of the defendant's fingerprints had been found in Debbie Carter's apartment. The blood samples did not match either of them and none of the patrons, who had been at the Coachlight, when interviewed, remembered seeing either of them on the night of the murder.

In the filmed interview with Williamson's mother in March of 1982, she told the police that Ron Williamson was at home with her by ten p.m. on December 7, 1982. Both Fritz and Williamson twice submitted to polygraph tests, which both of them passed and had twice given hair samples.

Ron Williamson had been without any medication for his mental disorders for several days after his arrest when he gave an interview to an OSBI agent and allegedly related a dream he had where he murdered Debbie Carter. Two weeks later, John Christian, an employee of the Pontotoc County Sheriff's office, said that Williamson had related a second dream in which he thought he murdered Carter.

After Barney Ward had been appointed as defense counsel for Williamson on June 1, 1987, he stated: "I had significant difficulties in dealing with Mr. Williamson. Mr. Williamson behaved well enough when I visited him at the jail, although I did hear stories from the jailers about incidents of unusual behavior. However, his conduct at court appearances was atrocious and unpredictable. At virtually every appearance, there was some kind of outburst from him. At the preliminary hearing, he became so incensed that he turned a table over on my secretary and Greg Saunders, counsel for Dennis Fritz. At that point, Mr. Williamson had to be removed from the courtroom.

The preliminary hearing lasted for several days and the judge gave Mr. Williamson more than one opportunity to return to the proceedings, but he always refused. As a result, he missed the entire preliminary hearing."

Oklahoma Statute Title 11, S 1175.2 reads: "No person shall be subject to any criminal procedures if he is determined to be incompetent. The question of the incompetence of a person may be raised by the person, or by the defense attorney by an application for determination of competency. The application for determination of competency shall allege that the person is incompetent to undergo further procedures and shall state facts sufficient to undergo further proceedings and shall state facts sufficient to raise a doubt as to the competency of the person."

Section 1175.1 defines "Criminal Proceedings" as: "Every stage of a criminal prosecution after arrest and before judgment, including, but not limited to, interrogation, lineup, preliminary hearing, motion dockets, discovery, pretrial hearings and trial; therefore, it is apparent counsel's obligation to initiate competency proceedings continues until judgment is entered, and failure to initiate a competency hearing may result in a deprivation of due process."

"When no state court competency hearing has been held and the defendant has proceeded to trial without such a hearing, the issue is not whether the state court record supports a finding of competency. Rather an inquiry on habeas is whether counsel denied the defendant his right to due process by ignoring evidence, including evidence at trial, indicating that the defendant might not be competent, and that a hearing to ascertain competency was therefore required. Evidence of defendant's demeanor is, of course, relevant in making this assessment because counsel's duty to inquire as to competency continues through trial."

Ward failed to request any competency hearing during this preliminary hearing, and Williamson was bound over for trial without incident.

On November 13, 1987, the preliminary hearing for Dennis Fritz, accused of first degree murder began.

District Attorney, Bill Peterson called two witnesses, Gary Wayne Allen, who claimed that he was a former neighbor of Fritz, and Mike Tinney, who was serving as an intern at he Pontotoc County jail during the past summer while Fritz was being held there.

When questioned by Peterson, Gary Allen testified that he saw Fritz and another man sometime between December 1, and December

10, 1982, 'raising cane and fighting with a water hose' around 3:30 a.m. He said he couldn't identify the other man with Fritz, but could see that they weren't wearing shirts.

When examined by defense attorney Greg Saunders, Allen said that the two men appeared to be 'shooting each other with a water hose' rather than washing off. He also admitted that he couldn't swear that it was Fritz who was involved in the incident. Allen said he told Ada assistant police chief, Dennis Smith about the water fight last summer when Fritz was arrested for the crime. Allen said he remembered the incident after looking through an old diary, but admitted that he didn't know the exact date it occurred.

Tinney, when called to the witness stand by Peterson, told the court about a conversation he had with Dennis Fritz in August at the Pontotoc County jail in which he had inquired about, 'making a deal'. Tinney said Fritz used the words 'what if maybe' in explaining a scenario in which Williamson broke into Carter's apartment, both of them 'got a little' and Williamson got 'carried away'. He said Fritz asked him how he could tell the district attorney when he didn't see Williamson do it.

When questioned by Saunders, however, Tinney admitted that Fritz had told him numerous times that he was innocent. He said that the conversation about Williamson could also have been another plea of innocence by Fritz.

Saunders then requested that the murder charge against Fritz be dismissed, arguing that the testimony of both witnesses and other evidence presented by the prosecution was not substantial enough to implicate his client in Carter's death.

Peterson argued that the testimony of the witnesses and hair samples found in Carter's apartment placed Fritz at the crime scene. He said some of the testimony presented at the preliminary hearing might not be admissible during a trial, but urged the judge to allow a jury to decide the case.

The judge said that he needed time to review transcripts from prior hearings before making a ruling for dismissal. He continued the hearing until 10:00 a.m. the following day.

On November 14, 1987, the judge ruled against Saunders's motion for dismissal.

On December 3, 1987, the Ada Evening News reported that a man whose name was Ricky Simmons (no relation to Gary E.

Simmons, Renee Williamson Simmons husband) had confessed to the murder of Debra Carter.

District Attorney, Peterson admitted that the Ada police had a videotaped confession by Simmons during a hearing for murder suspect Ron Williamson that was held several days before. This third suspect, the district attorney said, contacted the Ada Police Department and confessed to the crime two months earlier. However, he said, the man had a history of mental illness and was not a credible suspect. Peterson also said that investigators found no incriminating evidence against Simmons and could not implicate him in the murder.

He said that a local psychologist was treating Simmons. He further stated that Simmons provided few details in the crime and knew only what he had read and heard through the local media. Hair, blood and saliva samples were taken, Peterson said, and the test results did not implicate Simmons in the Carter murder

The morning after the article about the Ricky Simmons confession appeared in the Ada Evening News, the breakfast crowd at the Parkview expressed a variety of opinions regarding the upcoming trial.

"Well, what I want to know is this. If this Simmons boy is crazy like it says in this here newspaper, and he ain't competent enough to be tried for murder even if he's confessed, how come old Williamson can be tried when there's hard evidence he's been in the loony bin up there at the State Hospital a dozen times?"

"There wasn't any finger prints or nothing against that Simmons guy."

"There wasn't any finger prints against Williamson either. It just don't make sense to me. No finger prints that match, no blood matches, nobody seen them fellows anywhere close to that place where she lived and nobody seen them anywhere near that bar that night."

"They got some hair that might match."
"Hair?"
"That's what I heard. They can match hair."
"How much hair?"
"One or two hairs. It's some kind of science."
"I can't believe it. Convicting some poor son of a bitch because of a couple of hairs."

CHAPTER THIRTEEN

On April 6, 1988, the trial of Dennis Fritz began.

The Ada Evening News reported: "Jury selection began today in the trial of Dennis Fritz, accused of killing an Ada woman here more than five years ago.

Potential jurors crowded into the Pontotoc County District Courtroom this morning. The jury is expected to be seated today with District Judge Ron Jones presiding over the trial.

Fritz, 38, and Ron Williamson, 35, are charged with two counts of first-degree murder in the death of Debra Sue Carter. Her nude body was discovered in her garage apartment in Ada on December 8, 1982.

According to the medical examiner's report, Carter died of asphyxiation when a washcloth was stuffed down her throat. Ada police said the twenty-one year old woman had been beaten, raped and sodomized.

Williamson's trial is scheduled to begin on April 22, 1988, in Pontotoc County District Court.

Trials for both men had been set last December, but were postponed after a Pontotoc County grand jury was empanelled. Fritz was a junior high school teacher in Noble, Oklahoma, when Carter was murdered. He has claimed his innocence since being arrested for the crime last May in Kansas City, Missouri.
Carter was a graduate of Ada High School. At the time of her murder, she had been working at a local nightclub."

On April 7, 1988, the report from the Ada Evening News continued: "The testimony began today in Pontotoc County District Court in the murder trial of Dennis Fritz.

After opening statements by the state and defense, District Attorney Bill Peterson called his first witness, Glen Gore.

Gore testified that he was at the Coachlight Club where Carter was working part time as a bartender on the night of December 7, 1982. He said that she was talking to Ron Williamson in the club and she later told him (Gore) that Williamson was bothering her.

Gore testified that he did not see Fritz at the Coachlight that night.

Gina Vietta, who worked as a bartender at the Coachlight the night of December 7, 1982, testified that she had seen Fritz and Williamson there several times, but she did not recall either of them being at the club on December 7.

Vietta said that around four o'clock in the morning of December 8, Carter called her and said that she was frightened. She asked Vietta to come by and pick her up. Carter told her that someone was in her apartment, but she didn't mention any names. Then, after a minute or so, Carter told her that she would stay at her apartment that night, but asked her to call early in the morning and wake her up.

Charlie Carter testified that on the evening of December 8, 1982, he arrived at his daughter's apartment and found her nude body face down on the bedroom floor. The apartment, he said, had been ransacked."

On the second day of Dennis Fritz's trial, Dennis Smith, the detective who was the first to enter the Carter apartment after Charlie Carter called the police, told the court that the words, "Die" and "Duke" were written on Carter's body in fingernail polish and catsup. The color of the washcloth in her mouth was green. He reported that the words, "Don't look for us or elce", had been written on the kitchen table, with the obvious misspellings and the words, "Jim Smith next will die" were scrawled in fingernail polish on the living room wall.

Carter's torn panties were on the bedroom floor, Smith said, and officers found a catsup bottle wrapped in the bed sheets on the floor. He said an electric blanket cord and a leather belt with the name "Debbie" carved into it were around her neck. The blanket cord was later determined to have been the likely murder weapon. Smith said the police collected fingerprints, bed sheets, stuffed animals, clothing, broken glass from the front door window and hair samples from the apartment and this evidence was sent to the Oklahoma State Bureau of Investigation's crime lab for testing. He also testified that a piece of wall with a bloody palm print was removed and transferred to the OSBBI for analysis.

Saliva samples, along with head and pubic hairs were collected from all of Carter's known acquaintances and from patrons of the Coachlight Club. He said that Jim Smith and Duke Graham, who had police records, were investigated by officers, but were ruled out as suspects.

Smith said that Williamson became a prime suspect in March of 1983, after officers were told that Williamson beat up Robert Deatherage, when both were locked up in the Ada City Jail. Smith said Deatherage told police that Williamson became violent after he mentioned Carter's murder.

Smith said that Williamson, who lived with his mother on East 7th Street, about one block west of Carter's apartment, was interviewed by police about the crime in March of 1983. However, he said Williamson and his mother both maintained that he was at home the night Carter was murdered

Gary Rogers of the OSBI said Fritz had become a suspect when investigators learned that he and Williamson were friends and sometimes visited the Coachlight Club together. He said fingerprints, saliva and hair samples were also taken from Fritz in 1983.

Rogers also testified that he and the police were delayed in their investigation because the bloody print found in Carter's apartment did not appear to match prints of Williamson, Fritz or Carter. He said authorities feared that a third suspect might have been involved in the crime.

Rogers said Carter's parents authorized an exhumation of their daughter's body to allow investigators to take a full palm print. After further inspection, he said the OSBI determined that the print was indeed Carter's.

Rogers said he believed the crime was committed by two men, but admitted that it would have been possible for only one attacker to be involved.

Gary Allen, a former neighbor of Fritz, testified that he saw two men 'hosing each other down' with a water hose outside his house around 3:00 a.m. one morning between December 1 and December 10. He said he recognized the voice of one of the men as being Fritz, but couldn't identify the other man.

Allen said neither man was wearing a shirt, even though it was below freezing that morning. He said he didn't tell police about the incident until last summer, when both Fritz and Williamson were arrested.

William Kent Martin, superintendent of Noble Schools, testified that school records showed that Fritz, who was employed as a junior high school teacher and coach, had missed work the day Carter was slain. He said Fritz had missed four other days during the school year for illness.

James Harjo, who was held in The Pontotoc County Jail with Fritz last fall, described a conversation that he and Fritz allegedly had on Halloween night in the jail. He said Fritz told him that he was worried about Allen's testimony during his preliminary hearing. Harjo demonstrated how he diagramed on paper what Fritz told him and said he "figured out" that Fritz was guilty. When he confronted Fritz, Fritz began crying and told him, "We didn't mean to hurt her." Mike Tinney, a Pontotoc County jailer, also described a conversation that he and Fritz allegedly had last August. He said Fritz talked about a plea bargain with the district attorney's office, and explained a scenario in which Williamson had killed Carter.

When questioned by Fritz's attorney, Saunders, Tinney said Fritz had continued to claim his innocence of the murder. He said that the conversation about Williamson could have been another plea of innocence by Fritz.

On the second day of the trial, District Attorney Peterson questioned Cindy McIntosh, who was an inmate at the Pontotoc County Jail last fall. She described an alleged conversation she had heard between Fritz and Williamson. She testified she heard Williamson ask Fritz, who had seen photographs of Carter's body during his preliminary hearing, whether Carter was 'still on the floor or on the bed'. She said she didn't recall if Fritz had any response.

Jerry Peters, crime scene specialist for the OSBI, said he took photographs of the body and fingerprints of Carter. He said he compared the fingerprints with the evidence collected by the Ada police and the OSBI, including a bloody palm print on Carter's bedroom wall.

During his first analysis, Peters said he was unable to determine the identity of the print because of the condition of the deceased's hands. However, after Carter's body was exhumed last spring, he identified the prints as being hers.

Peters said none of the prints taken from Carter's apartment matched prints taken from Fritz or Williamson.

Mary Long, criminalist for the OSBI, said she had examined body fluids collected from Carter's body and other evidence collected from the apartment. She said that semen samples taken from the body revealed that the assailant or assailants were non-secretors and did not secret blood in their bodily fluids. As a result, she said, the blood type of the attacker could not be determined.

Long explained that about twenty per cent of the population can be classified as non-secretors. From her tests, she concluded that both Fritz and Williamson were non-secretors.

She said she also believed Carter was a non-secretor. When questioned by defense attorney, Greg Saunders, Long admitted that eleven of the nineteen suspects who submitted saliva samples to the OSBI could also have been non-secretors. However, she admitted that not all of those suspects were given blood tests.

When Dennis Fritz took the witness stand, he denied any involvement in the killing of Debbie Carter more than five years ago. When questioned by defense attorney Greg Saunders, Fritz told the jury that he did not kill Carter. He said he never knew Carter, had never been in her apartment and had not raped her on the night she was killed.

Fritz said he read about Carter's murder in a newspaper, and was shocked that the crime had occurred at an apartment only six blocks from his mother's home on 8th Street.

He stated that he was a graduate of Southeastern University in Durant, Oklahoma and that he taught school at Konawa during the fall of 1981, but resigned before the end of the school term in August of 1982. He said he became a junior high school teacher and coach in August of 1982 in Noble, Oklahoma.

Fritz said that he lived in a trailer on the school grounds in Noble, but returned to Ada on the weekends to visit his mother and his daughter, Elizabeth. He said he spent most of his time in Noble, but occasionally traveled to Ada during the week. He testified that he met Williamson in the fall of 1981, when Williamson was playing a guitar outside a local convenience store and they became friends and 'ran around together' when he was in Ada.

In March of 1983, Fritz said the Ada police questioned him about the Carter murder. He said he cooperated with the investigation, but repeatedly denied any involvement in the case. Fritz said the Noble school system fired him in the spring of 1983, after Ada police notified school officials about a prior felony conviction against him and told them of their murder investigation. He said he returned to Ada where he worked construction until he moved to his mother's home in Kansas City, Missouri, where she moved with Elizabeth after the notification that Dennis was a suspect in the Carter murder.

Fritz said that jailer, Mike Tinney continually advised him to plea bargain with the district attorney's office, but he told Tinney he was innocent. "I told him if I was guilty and had been there, don't you think I would make some kind of deal. Do you think I would go through all this?"

Fritz also denied admitting his involvement in the crime to James Harjo, who was being held in the Pontotoc County Jail with Fritz last fall. He said he had helped Harjo write letters to his family and he thought they had become friends until Harjo accused him of killing Carter one night.

After ordering Harjo out of his cell, Fritz said Harjo threatened to 'make up something as pure as gold' to tell authorities and damage his case.

When questioned by District Attorney Peterson, Fritz admitted that he lied on two job applications, a teacher's certificate, and several pawn shop documents about his felony conviction in 1973. He said he had been convicted of cultivation of marijuana, but failed to disclose the information to school officials at Konawa and Noble.

Fritz said he occasionally provided transportation for Williamson, but had never driven him to the Coachlight Club, where Carter worked. He said he had visited the club only a few times. He said that he couldn't remember where he was the night of the Carter murder, but told officers that he could have been at a girlfriend's house.

"I just know where I wasn't," he said.

Earlier, Melvin Hett, a forensic chemist for the OSBI, testified that hairs found in Carter's apartment were compared to samples submitted by suspects in the case. He said the hairs were compared for various characteristics, including color, cuticle thickness, scale damage and abnormalities.

Hett said his research revealed that eleven pubic and two scalp hairs collected at the crime scene were 'consistent microscopically' with those of Fritz and 'could have the same source'. He added that two scalp hairs were also consistent with those of Williamson. Questioned by Saunders, Hett admitted that hair comparison was a 'somewhat subjective science' and could not be used for positive identification. He also said that it would be possible for experts in the field to disagree on the results of hair comparison.

On the last day of the Fritz trial, defense attorney, Saunders, called Richard Brisbane, a forensic expert from Chicago to the witness stand.

Brisbane testified that he had examined pubic hairs found in the Carter apartment and compared them with those of Fritz in February. He said he determined only three of the pubic hairs collected from the crime scene were similar to those of Fritz. Brisbane's findings contradicted the testimony from Hett, the forensic chemist from the OSBI. Brisbane said it is possible for more than one person to have the same hair characteristics, and researchers occasionally cannot distinguish hair from two different sources. As a result, he said, hair comparison cannot be used for positive identification.

In his closing argument, Saunders told the jury that the State had failed to present sufficient evidence implicating Fritz in the murder. He said testimony from the State's witnesses attempted to establish a tie between Fritz and Williamson, and that the prosecution was seeking guilt only by association.

Peterson argued that earlier testimony from witnesses proved that Fritz and Williamson were partners in the crime. He said evidence from the hair comparison show that both Fritz and Williamson visited Carter's apartment the night she was killed. Peterson was seeking the death penalty for Fritz, but the jurors had the sentence options of death, imprisonment for life and life imprisonment without parole.

Shortly after 11:00 a.m., the jury announced that it lacked one vote to recommend a sentence in the case. The jurors were summoned back into the courtroom and Peterson called Levita Brewer, Oklahoma City, to the witness stand. Brewer testified that Fritz and Williamson abducted her from a nightclub parking lot in Norman, Oklahoma in 1983, and kept her in their vehicle while speeding through city streets.

Brewer said she begged them to let her out, but they refused to release her from the vehicle. Finally, she said, she jumped from the moving vehicle, ran from the area and telephoned the police.

Peterson told the jurors to recommend the death penalty for Fritz. Staring at Fritz, he said, "Jurors should say to him, Dennis Fritz, you deserve to die for what you did."

Interrupting Peterson, Fritz looked at the jury and said, "I did not kill Debbie Carter."

After deliberating for several hours, the jury requested additional testimony from Richard Brisbane, the forensic expert from Chicago. Judge Jones denied their request and ordered them to continue deliberating until they reached a decision.

At 6:00 p.m., the jury was brought back into the courtroom by Judge Jones, but the jury foreman told him they still had not reached a verdict and were split eleven to one. Jones sent the jurors out again and told them to review the evidence and reach a verdict.

The jury finally announced its guilty verdict about 8:15 p.m. and recommended a sentence of life without parole.

As Dennis Fritz was being led back to the Pontotoc County Jail, the victim's mother, Peggy, fainted on the lawn outside the courthouse. She was treated by ambulance attendants from Valley View Hospital but was later released.

CHAPTER FOURTEEN

On the morning to April 13, 1988, the Parkview was packed with customers. The smoke from the kitchen where bacon and sausage sizzled on the grille, mixed with the thin vapors curling upward from the ashtrays on the Formica topped tables.

"Well, I'm damn glad the whole thing is about to be finished."

"Was you at the courthouse yesterday when they brought in the verdict?"

"Was working yesterday."

"If you had a been there you would have seen a sight."

"How'd Dennis take it?"

"Not good. Just hung his head."

"You think he done it?"

"Don't know. Don't think them people on the jury knows neither."

"How come?"

"I been there all week watching the trial."

"Must be nice not to have nothing better to do than watch some poor guy get fried."

"Hey, man, I earned that pension. Worked every day for damn near forty-five years and earned every penny. Anyway, Dennis ain't going to fry."

"Ron will."

"Probably."

"Guess we'll see next week. Or you will, since you got nothing better to do."

"You can read the newspaper."

"Don't need to since I got you here every morning to report what happened."

"You're a lucky man to have me around to explain things."

"I'd be luckier if I had a pension like you."

Agnes cleared the last of the dishes from the tables and stacked them on the pass-through window to the kitchen.

"You think he done it?" she asked the cook.

"Don't know."

"What about the other one?"

The cook shrugged his shoulders.

"You know either one of them boys?" she asked.

He shook his head. "Never come in here that I can remember."

"This ain't one of their hang outs."

"I guess this crowd's too old for 'em. What we got here is a bunch of philosophers."

"What's that?"

"Old folks that sit around and talk about things they don't know nothing about."

"Well, we got them all right."

CHAPTER FIFTEEN

The morning of April 21, 1988, the sky was dark, with low clouds and the weather forecasters warned of heavy rain and the possibility of tornados in the area. The group of people who had been called for possible jury selection brought umbrellas and raincoats into the courtroom. A jury was expected to be seated by the end of the day for the murder trial of Ronald Keith Williamson.

The Ada Evening News gave a full report of Williamson's arrest almost eleven months ago. Fritz, the report continued, was still in the Pontotoc County Jail since his conviction several days before of murder in the first degree and given a life sentence

Both men were originally charged with first-degree rape and rape by instrumentation, but those charges were dropped at a July preliminary hearing. Defense attorneys successfully argued that the three-year time limit for filing such charges had expired.

The newspaper report also stated that Williamson disrupted his preliminary hearing by yelling obscenities at Fritz and loudly declaring his own innocence. He was removed from the courtroom and did not attend the majority of his preliminary hearing.

The jury was seated in the late afternoon of April 21, and the trial began the following morning with District Judge Ron Jones presiding.

Assistant District Attorney, Nancy Shew, gave the opening statement and called Glen Gore as the first witness. Gore refused to answer any questions from the court and was asked if he knew what would happen to him if he did not testify.

"Do you know what will happen to me if I do testify?" he replied. "If this court wishes to find me in contempt, you should do so at this time."

After a discussion with Shew and Williamson's attorney, William B. 'Barney' Ward, District Judge Jones decided to use Gore's testimony from Williamson's preliminary hearing, and went over the transcript while the jury, which consisted of five women and seven men, were recessed.

Ward objected to the use of the transcript, but after a discussion between the judge and the attorneys, it was decided that the transcript would be read to the jury. The jury was recalled to the courtroom and Gore's testimony was read.

Gore testified at the preliminary hearing that he was at an Ada nightclub the night before Carter's death, when a man named Ron asked him if he wanted to go to the Coachlight Club for a drink. A little before 1:30 a.m., he said he saw Ron talking to Debbie Carter. Carter then asked Gore, "Would you rescue me?" so he danced with her. Gore stated that he did not see Fritz at the Coachlight Club that night.

Tommy Glover testified he knew Carter because he had worked with her at Brockway Glass Company and he knew she worked part time at the Coachlight Bar. He testified he was at the club the night of December 7th. He said he didn't see Carter in the club, but did see her talking to Gore while standing by her car in the parking lot. He said he left and didn't see whether Carter left by herself or with someone.

Gina Vietta testified she also worked at the Coachlight Club as a waitress and she knew Williamson and Fritz. She said they came to the bar sometimes as much as three times a week. About two or three weeks before Carter's death, Vietta said Carter asked to trade working stations with her because Williamson was at her station and was making her uncomfortable. Vietta said she did not remember if she saw Williamson or Fritz at the Coachlight the night before Carter's death

Vietta then was questioned about a phone call she received from Carter in the early morning hours of December 8th. Carter told her there was someone there and she didn't feel comfortable with him. She wanted Vietta to come and pick her up. Vietta said she heard a muffled sound like someone put a hand over the phone mouthpiece. They hung up and a few minutes later, Carter called her back and said, "Never mind".

Gary Allen told the jury that he had lived in an apartment behind the house where Fritz was living. Sometime between December 1 and December 10, 1982, he was awakened early in the morning by laughing and cursing outside his apartment. He said he looked out and saw two men with a water hose. They apparently were spraying each other. Allen stated that he couldn't see the men well enough to recognize them, but did recognize one of the voices. He testified that he thought it was Fritz.

Charlie Carter, Debbie's father, told the jury about finding her body. He found her apartment door standing open and her nude body, clad only in a pair of white socks, on her bedroom floor. He told the jury, "I had the authorities notified but I knew she was dead. Everything looked out of place, like there had been a big fight."

Retired assistant police chief, Dennis Smith, testified about his role in the investigation beginning with the day of the incident. Officers secured the scene, checked door to door for possible witnesses and began collecting evidence.

During Smith's testimony about the crime scene, Williamson cried and hung his head.

Smith also described the procedure of how hair and saliva samples were collected from defendants Williamson and Fritz. Doctor Fred Jordan, the medical examiner and pathologist for the OSBI, said he conducted the autopsy on Carter, and ruled that she died of asphyxiation from a washcloth being stuffed down her throat and a ligature pulled around her neck.

Jordan said Carter appeared to have been beaten, and he believed that she was alive when the wounds and bruises were inflicted on her body. Photographs, showing the bruises and the writings on Carter's body were distributed to the jurors during Jordan's testimony.

Questioned by defense attorney, Barney Ward, Jordan said semen found in Carter's body had been deposited between twenty-four and thirty-six hours before he received her body at his laboratory in Oklahoma City.

Tony Vick testified that he had lived in an apartment behind Dennis Fritz from late 1981 until February 1983. He stated he had seen Williamson and Fritz together on many occasions. He said that he had seen them together many times at the Coachlight Club.

Donna Walker, a former employee at Love's Country Store in Ada, told the jury she remembered Williamson and Fritz as customers in the store. She testified that they came into the store together, sometimes several times a day. She stated that after the death of Carter, she noticed that Fritz and Williamson began to look unkempt. They wore dirty clothes and were unshaven. She also noticed a difference in their personalities. They became belligerent and hateful, Walker said.

A former schoolmate of Williamson's, Letha Caldwell Morris testified about how Williamson approached her while she was jogging in Matthews Park in the spring of 1983. She stated that he and Fritz would come to her house at late hours of the night together. When attorney Ward asked her what kind of car they were driving, she said she didn't know.

Terri Holland, a former Pontotoc County jail inmate, testified about a conversation she overheard Williamson have with his mother, Holland said he told his mother to bring him some stuff. He said if she didn't bring him what he wanted, he would kill her just like he did Debbie Carter. She also told the jury about things she overheard Williamson say. She told about Williamson saying he wanted to go with Debbie Carter, but she wouldn't go with him. She said he said he wouldn't have had to kill her if she would have just gone along.

At this point, Williamson stood up and shouted, "She's a liar! I never killed anybody in my life!" On two different occasions, deputies and detectives had to calm Williamson. At one point, Williamson told Holland, "You are lying. You'll have to pay for that."

Ward then asked Holland whether or not she believed Williamson and she said she did not.

Judge Jones cautioned Williamson to remain calm or he would be taken from the courtroom.

Another former jail inmate, Cindy McIntosh, testified that she overheard Williamson ask Fritz, after Fritz had seen pictures of the crime scene, "Was she on the floor or on the bed?"

Two Pontotoc County Sheriff's Department employees testified about information Williamson had told them. Jailer Mike Tinney told the jury that Williamson told him that, "Gore was confused about what he saw at the Coachlight that night. No one saw me sneak up the stairs and break her door in."

Sheriff Deputy John Christian testified that Williamson and he were school classmates. He said while in jail Williamson told him, "Just imagine this. I was living in Tulsa, taking Quaaludes and drinking beer. I came to Ada and went to the Coachlight Club and met Debbie Carter. I went to her place, knocked on the door and she said, 'hold on' because she was on the phone. I went in, raped and killed her."

Christian also said Williamson told him about wanting to get on a bus and travel around. Williamson said he figured that's what the killer did.

On the third day of the trial, Melvin Hett, crime specialist for the OSBI, presented graphs of hair samples before the court, describing the characteristics of human hair and explaining the science of hair comparison.

Hett said he spent several hundred hours studying known and unknown hair samples in the case. He said he determined that pubic and scalp hairs from both Williamson and Fritz were "microscopically consistent" with hairs found at the crime scene.

Hett also said none of the hairs submitted by other suspects in the case were consistent with those gathered at the crime scene. However, he admitted that hair comparison could not be used for positive identification.

The State rested its case after Hett's testimony.

Williamson's attorney, Barney Ward, waived his right to an opening statement and called his first witness. He called seven employees or former employees of the Pontotoc County Jail. Each of the seven testified they had never heard Williamson make any comments, incriminating or otherwise, while at the jail.

Ward also had court clerk Wayne Joplin testify to the records of an earlier witness. Ward wanted to discredit Terri Holland's testimony. Williamson had become extremely upset by jail inmate Holland's testimony regarding his conversation with his mother.

At several points in the testimony given by Holland, Williamson had to be calmed by the deputies as well as his sister, Annette Hudson. Ward told him, "Be quiet now and let me do the talking."

OSBI crime scene specialist, Jerry Peters told about fingerprints taken at the crime scene. He said the only prints that were identifiable were those of Carter, Ada detective Dennis Smith and one other individual who was not a suspect in the case.

Peters told the jury Carter's body was ordered to be exhumed when he discovered that the bloody palm print found on the bedroom wall of Carter's apartment had never been identified. However, he stated, the palm print was identified as being that of Carter.

Two of the OSBI criminalists, Mary Long and Susan Land, explained the difficulty of determining the identity by using saliva samples from individuals who were non-secretors, which she believed both Williamson and Fritz were, because they do not secrete blood into their body fluids. She added that she believed Debbie Carter was a non-secretor as well.

Land told the jury that her job was to collect hair samples, mount them on slides and then turn them over to Melvin Hett for his analysis.

The last day of Williamson's trial began with District Attorney Peterson's closing argument to the jury.

While describing the testimony of witness Terri Holland, Peterson told about a phone call Holland allegedly heard between Williamson and his mother. Peterson reminded the jury of what Holland had said. "Bring the stuff or I'll kill you like I did Debbie Carter".

At this point, Williamson shouted out, "Mr. Peterson, shut your mouth! I never said that!"

During a recess, Williamson was standing in the hall and declared to Carter's father, "Mr. Carter, I did not kill your daughter." Williamson was very upset and had to be taken back into the courtroom.

Before the jury was brought back into the courtroom after this recess, Williamson told his sister he did not want to stay in the courtroom while Peterson finished his closing remarks regarding Holland's testimony because it wasn't the truth. Hudson warned her brother not to talk, to think about the Bible and try to block out Peterson's remarks.

The jury was given the case to deliberate at 10:15 a.m. on April 28, 1988. At 10:40 a.m., it came back into the courtroom with a question about photographs of the crime scene and of Debbie Carter's body.

The jury deliberated until 12:30 p.m., took a one-hour lunch break and then returned with their verdict at 4:40 p.m.

Before that verdict was read, Judge Jones reminded Williamson and the rest of the courtroom that any type of response after the verdict was read could mean a contempt of court charge. The crowd remained quiet as court clerk Wayne Joplin read the guilty verdict. Williamson hung his head, his sister cried and Carter's mother cried. Some of the female jurors also cried quietly

Assistant District Attorney, Nancy Shew then gave her opening statement for the sentencing phase of the trial. She briefed the jury on testimony they would hear from four witnesses. The first witness called was Beverly Steliff.

Setliff testified that in June 1981, she was getting ready for bed. She heard a voice outside her window that she thought was her neighbor. When she pulled back the shade, she saw the face of a man she didn't know, but later discovered was Williamson. Setliff told the jury that she ran to the phone to call a friend and could hear the latch being pulled from her back door. The person outside the window was not found. She later pointed out Williamson to a friend who identified him.

Levita Brewer told the jury about an incident that involved Williamson and Fritz. In 1982, she was at a motel nightclub in Norman, Oklahoma. Fritz approached her, and asked her to dance. They danced a couple of times and when the club closed, she started to leave. When she walked out the front door of the club, Fritz pulled his car up to the door and Williamson was in the passenger seat. Fritz asked her to look at a portable bar he had in his car and when she sat on the back seat, he drove off. She jumped from the car when it slowed down. She ran between houses and alleyways until she could find a pay phone.

Letha Caldwell Morris, who had testified in the trial, also said that Williamson and Fritz would come to her house at all hours of the night. They usually had been drinking and offered her pills.
She testified that Williamson came in her house in late 1982. She was working in her yard and he sat on her porch and drank beer. He wanted her to stop working and talk to him, but when she refused, he grabbed her by the wrist and threw her against the house. She broke away from him and he eventually left.

Andrea Hardcastle testified that Williamson and an acquaintance of hers came to her house one night and asked her to go to the Coachlight Club. She refused because she was babysitting and because her ex-husband was a bouncer at the club. The pair left and she noticed Williamson had left his cigarettes. When she returned to the living room, Williamson had entered the house.

Hardcastle told the jury the defendant told her he wanted her to have sex with him and when she refused, he knocked her to the floor. She testified that he ripped the inside of her mouth by shoving his fingers inside her mouth and he beat her with his fist and open hand. She said that Williamson wanted her to say, "I love you." When she refused, he hit her again. She finally said that she loved him because she feared for her life. The witness explained other sexual acts Williamson allegedly wanted her to perform.

"If I could get him to talk, he would calm down and then he would go into a rage again and start hitting me. He wouldn't let me out of arms length and I couldn't get to a phone. Close to the end of the ordeal," she said, "he sat on my chest and said, 'you know I'm going the have to kill you, don't you?'.

She said she had already made peace with God, because she knew that he was going to kill her, however Williamson left after she promised him that she wouldn't tell anyone.

Hardcastle's father contacted the police when he discovered that incident, but she refused to file charges when she became aware that Williamson lived only two houses away from her.

The jury of five women and seven men recommended a sentence of death.

After the proceedings ended, Carter's father said he wanted to thank everyone who helped with the case because they had worked so hard during the past five years. He stated, "I would have said the same thing if the verdict had been different."

Carter's mother, Peggy, and her sister Darla Tatum, said they were pleased with the decision of the jury. "We are proud that justice was done," they said. The two also asked for Debbie's respect.

Peterson said, "The jury did their duty. They reached the appropriate verdict and sentence, and I'm satisfied."

Williamson made only two comments during the day's proceedings. Both times he proclaimed his innocence. He was never unruly and was taken back to the county jail without incident.

On April 29, 1988, the morning after Ron Williamson's trial, Agnes, for the first time in the twelve years she had worked at the Parkview, was late for work.

"You sick?" the cook asked.

"Couldn't sleep."

"Yeah, I saw the news last night."

"What you think it's like being on death row?"

The cook shook his head.

"Lonesome, I'll bet."

"Probably sees his lawyer."

"Why? The trial's over."

"Appeals. He can ask for appeals."

"Don't seem to me his lawyer wants to have much to do with him."

"Just because he had his son sitting as a bodyguard behind him carrying a blackjack don't mean he didn't want to help Ron. That lawyer's blind you know, and he's getting old. Ron would have been a handful."

"Did you say his son was carrying a blackjack?"

"Told the boy if Ron got violent to whack him and if he killed Ron, not to worry cause he could get him off."

"Good Lord."

Agnes took the donuts from the morning before from the pie case and put them in a box. "I'll put these out back for Floyd when he comes by."

The cook nodded.

"Wonder what the jail has for breakfast."

"Probably not too bad here at the county jail, but up there at the state pen – maybe not so good."

"I'm just glad its over."

"Believe me, Agnes," the cook said, "It's not over yet."

On May 19, 1988, Judgment and Sentence on Conviction was filed in the District Court of Pontotoc County, Oklahoma. The following morning, Ronald Keith Williamson and Dennis Leon Fritz were transferred to the Oklahoma State Penitentiary in McAlester, Oklahoma, commonly known as "Big Mac".

Debbie Carter Yearbook photo 1982
Ada Evening News

Glen Gore at the time of his arrest for kidnapping 1987
Ada Evening News

Ron Williamson at his trial for murder 1988
Ada Evening News

Dennis Fritz, Teacher, 1982 Noble Oklahoma Yearbook
Ada Evening News

Dennis Fritz at his trial in 1988
Ada Evening News

Dennis Fritz Mug shot 1988
Ada Evening News

Fritz and Williamson react as Judge Landrith announces their freedom. Elizabeth Fritz (lower left) sees her father for the first time in twelve years.
Associated Press Photo

Williamson and Fritz at the gathering of friends after their release. Mother of Dennis Fritz in the background.
Associated Press Photo

Williamson enjoys a cigarette after his release at the Ada, Oklahoma courthouse.
Associated Press Photo

Glen Gore after his sentencing trial 2003
Ada Evening News

CHAPTER SIXTEEN

"I don't think I ever read a book
from cover to cover in my life
before they sent me up here to Big Mac.

Now I don't do nothin' else.

My daughter sends 'em to me,
reg'lar as clock work,
one ever' month.
nuthin' else, just a book.

I won't let her come up here
to see me.

No sir, I don't want her up here."

                Bedrock
       Images From the Wayside

    Dennis Fritz banned his daughter, Elizabeth, from coming to the prison to visit him. He vowed never to give up hope that one day he would be able to prove his innocence and would be vindicated. He told his mother that this was a place no thirteen year-old girl should experience. Elizabeth firmly supported her father and they kept in touch by phone and photographs. The visiting room, more often than not, was a scene of sexual intimacies and desperation – no place for his Elizabeth, Dennis said.
    An appeal is a request to a higher court to review and overturn the decision of a lower court. If an appeal is granted, an appellate court will review it.
    The appellate court in the State of Oklahoma is the Court of Criminal Appeals. This court will not conduct a new trial or look at new evidence, but will review the record in the transcripts of the trial proceedings. The person appealing must present a "brief" which is a written argument outlining what mistakes were made at trial and the laws that support the claimant's position.

Incarcerated prisoners are entitled to certain legal rights. They have access to the legal system, access to a law library where they may research the law and prepare motions in order to end their imprisonment.

Indigent defendants have not always enjoyed the privilege of court appointed counsel. A landmark case, Gideon v. Wainright, decided by the U.S. Supreme Court on March 18, 1963, granted this right. In this defendant's trial in a Florida State Court on a charge of a felony, this trial court denied defendant's request to appoint counsel for him on the ground that under the laws of Florida, only a defendant charged with a capital offense was entitled to such an appointment. After his conviction, defendant filed in the Supreme Court of Florida the present habeas corpus petition, attacking his conviction on the ground that his federal constitutional rights were violated by the trial court's refusal to appoint counsel.

On certiorari, the Supreme Court of the United States reversed, overruling Belts v. Brady, wherein it had been held that due process of law does not require that in every case, regardless of circumstances, an indigent accused must be furnished counsel by the State. The opinion of Justice Black, which expressed the views of seven members of the Court, it was held that the Sixth Amendment's provision that in all criminal prosecutions the accused shall enjoy the right to have the assistance of counsel for his defense was made obligatory upon the States by the Fourteenth Amendment.

Upon exhausting their appeals in state court, defendants may also file a petition for writ of habeas corpus in federal court for a review of the legality of their imprisonment. A prisoner may also ask the U.S. Supreme Court to review the highest state court or a lower federal court's decision by filing a writ of certiorari, but not all such applications are granted. In fact, only a few which raise important constitutional issues are ever considered by the U. S. Supreme Court. In U.S. v. Brady, another important decision by the U.S. Supreme Court required the government to provide any exculpatory evidence it has.

To establish a Brady violation, a defendant must establish that the prosecution suppressed evidence that was favorable to him or exculpatory and that the evidence was material. A finding of materiality is required under Brady. Materiality turns on the specific circumstances surrounding the alleged Brady violation. The U.S. Supreme Court has established a single test for materiality in those cases where the defense makes a specific request, a general request or no request for Brady material:

"The evidence is material only if there is a reasonable probability that, had the evidence been disclosed to the defense, the result of the proceeding would have been different. A 'reasonable probability' is a probability sufficient to undermine confidence in the outcome."

To find reversible error, the appellant must meet the burden of showing (1) the prosecution has actually suppressed evidence after that evidence has been requested by the defense; (2) the evidence was favorable to appellant's defense; and (3) the evidence is material either to the guilt of appellant or to his punishment.

Dennis Fritz knew how to use the prison library and from the time of his incarceration in May of 1988, he acted as his own attorney inside the prison walls. Fritz tried for several years to get the appellate courts to grant permission to conduct DNA tests on the physical evidence used to convict him. However, the court motions made on his behalf were denied. It was not until early in 1991, Fritz was able to file his appeal before the Court of Criminal Appeals.

Fritz's defense at trial was that Ronald Williamson acted alone in the murder of Debbie Carter. Therefore, evidence that Williamson had committed the same type of offense in the past, as was illustrated by his attack on Andrea Hardcastle, was material information that, Fritz argued, he was entitled to and was necessary to adequately cross-examine the investigative officers at to why they focused attention on Fritz.

The court disagreed and stated that the record shows that Andrea Hardcastle was endorsed as a witness on September 21, 1987, approximately seven months prior to trial. The evidence of the attack suffered by her at the hands of Williamson, a report prepared by the OSBI detectives, was turned over to the defense at the sentencing hearing and made a part of the record at that time.

The court stated that the State did not err by failing to turn over the report, as it did not fall into any of the categories of evidence ordered by the court to be turned over to Appellant Fritz prior to trial. It was neither a sworn statement nor a technical report. Neither was it exculpatory to Fritz as it illustrated only Williamson's violent tendencies toward women. Rather, it was a report prepared by the OSBI as part of their investigation and was therefore, the work product of the State. Appellant Fritz is not entitled to discovery of the State's work product. There is no constitutional requirement that the prosecution make a complete and detailed accounting to the defense of all police investigations on a case.

Further, the report was not material to Fritz's defense as it was cumulative of the first stage testimony of Letha Caldwell-Morris, who testified that Williamson, accompanied by Fritz, visited her home several times late at night. She stated that the actions of the two men and the way they talked scared her. She told them several times not to come back to her home and was finally forced to show them a gun in order to persuade them to stop bothering her.

Appellant Fritz's argument that the evidence was necessary to cross-examine the investigative officers is untenable, the Court stated. Agent Rogers testified on direct examination that his investigation initially led to Williamson and the information concerning a relationship between Fritz and Williamson. The existence of a report concerning Williamson's violent past would not have furthered Fritz's cross- examination of Rogers.

Based upon the foregoing, the Court said they did not find error in the State's failure to turn over the report concerning Williamson's attack on Hardcastle as such report was not exculpatory and production could not have substantially affected the outcome of the trial.

Fritz also alleged error in the failure of the State to turn over the report of Melvin Hett, dated April 7, 1988. During the sentencing hearing, the prosecutor stated that he did not receive the report until the Williamson trial, which occurred approximately one month after Fritz's trial.

The disputed report did not relate to Fritz's hair analysis, but merely excluded suspects Glen Gore and Rickey Simmons. Further, Fritz had access to the test results concerning the analysis of his hair samples as Agent Hett sent those results to Richard Brisbane, the defense expert witness, and received on February 25, 1988. As the report from Agent Hett was not exculpatory, and was not received by the State until after Fritz's trial, it was not error for the State to deliver a copy of the report to the defense prior to Appellant Fritz's trial. Fritz further contended that he was denied access to a videotape of his polygraph examination. He asserted that he was repeatedly denied access to the tape, despite his personal requests to the State and the Court's order for production. In his defense, the District Attorney stated at the sentencing hearing that the tape had been in his personal possession and no request had ever been made to him for the tape. The tape was ordered turned over to the Appellant Fritz at the sentencing hearing. The record does not reflect an objection at trial by Fritz to the omission of the tape nor was the need for the tape brought to the attention of the trial court.

The Court stated that evidence of Fritz's statement during the course of a polygraph examination, wherein he denies complicity in a crime, is exculpatory to the defense. However, we do not find the evidence in the present case material to the Appellant Fritz's involvement in the crime. No reasonable probability exists that, had the tape been provided to the defense prior to trial, the tape would have been admissible as to evidence or that the outcome of the trial would have been different.

In his second assignment of error, Fritz contended that he was denied a fair trial by prosecutorial misconduct during the closing argument. The record reflects that Fritz failed to enter contemporaneous objections at trial to the remarks now regarded as error. It is well established that the failure to object at trial to the closing arguments claimed as error constitutes a waiver of error unless it is fundamental.

During closing argument, the prosecutors referred to Fritz as 'an admitted liar' and commented on certain lies that he had told. These remarks were based upon the testimony of Fritz who stated he had lied on his job applications to Konawa and Noble Schools. While we, the Court, do not usually condone such name-calling, in the present case the remarks were reasonable comments on the evidence, which put into question the credibility of the Appellant Fritz. As the evidence supported these comments, we do not find that fundamental error occurred.

Fritz contended that the prosecutor improperly attacked defense counsel by indicating that counsel had fabricated a story that the victim fought for her life against only one assailant. Defense counsel objected to the comment and the trial court, sustained the objection in part, admonished the jury as follows:

"Ladies and gentlemen of the jury, credibility of the evidence that you have heard is not for attorneys in this case, and there is wide latitude in discussing the evidence, but it is for you to determine credibility, and personal opinion by counsel are not a part of this case."

We find that any error was cured by the admonishment Appellant Fritz further alleged that the prosecutor improperly argued facts not in evidence. When the prosecutor briefly referred to other cases that he had prosecuted, defense counsel objected. The objection was sustained and the jury admonished that other cases tried by the district attorney were not a part of the present case and that they were not to be influenced by his statement.

Appellant Fritz also contended that the prosecutor went outside the record in discussing the hair evidence. The argument that the prosecutor attempted to put before the jury was that the evidence showed that it was Fritz and Williamson who showed up at the decedent's apartment because "the likelihood of two people randomly meeting each other out in the world and getting together and going to the decedent's is almost incredible." However, before he could finish his statement, defense counsel objected and a long bench conference ensued. The trial court sustained the objection, ruling that the prosecutor could not make that argument to the jury, as it was an improper comment on the testimony of the expert witness. The prosecutor then resumed his closing on a different topic. We, the Court, find that no fundamental error occurred.

Other instances in which Fritz alleged the prosecutor went outside the record either drew no objection from the defense counsel or were objected to and the objection sustained and the jury admonished. Again, we have reviewed the comments and find that no fundamental error occurred.

Finally, Appellant Fritz contends that the prosecutor's attempt to introduce photographs of the decedent's exhumed body demonstrated the prosecution's "utter disregard for justice and his obsession with conviction at all costs." The record shows that Appellant Fritz objected to the attempted introduction of the evidence and the objection was sustained. The photographs were introduced during the testimony of the medical examiner and offered into evidence to substantiate that testimony concerning the testing performed on the decedent's palm in order to match the palm print found on the wall of the decedent's apartment. Therefore, a logical basis existed for the attempted introduction. However, no error occurred as the defense's objection was sustained and the jury never saw the photographs (wherein the Court finds no authority requiring reversal in a situation where the objection was sustained). Having reviewed Appellant's allegations of prosecutorial misconduct, we find that the complained remarks did not affect the outcome of this trial and that they neither separately nor cumulatively warrant modification or reversal. Accordingly, Appellant was not denied a fair trial by the conduct or remarks of the prosecutor and this assignment is without merit.

Fritz contended in his third assignment of error that the evidence was insufficient to sustain a verdict of guilty. Though the State's case against Appellant consisted almost entirely of circumstantial evidence, such evidence will be sufficient if the circumstances are "inconsistent with any reasonable hypothesis other than the defendant's guilt. The circumstantial evidence need not exclude every conceivable hypothesis or negate any possibility other than guilt. The evidence will be considered in the light most favorable to the State.

The Court of Criminal Appeals, Judge Lumpkin, Vice Presiding Judge, held that (1) prosecution's failure to turn over to defendant the report concerning co-defendant's prior attacks on women was not a Brady violation; (2) evidence was sufficient to convict for first-degree murder; and (3) delay between commission of crime and charge of murder being filed did not deprive defendant of a speedy trial.

Accordingly, for the foregoing reasons, the judgment and sentence of the trial court is AFFIRMED.
LANE, P.J., and BRETT and JOHNSON, J.J., concur.
PARKS, J., specially concur.
Dennis Leon Fritz, Appellant v State of Oklahoma, Appellee
Court of Criminal Appeals of Oklahoma – May 15, 1991
Rehearing Denied – July 5, 1991

Dennis Fritz was not without counsel at this hearing. His attorney was Rolando Davila, who before he went into private practice clerked for the Court of Criminal Appeals while a student in law school. Ronald Williamson, whose appeal was also filed May 15, 1991, was represented by William H. Luker, Assistant Appellate Public Defender, Norman, Oklahoma.

Robert H. Henry Attorney General for the State of Oklahoma was assisted by A. Diane Hammons in the hearing before the Court in the case of Dennis Fritz. In the hearing for Ronald Williamson, he was assisted by David Walling.

CHAPTER SEVENTEEN

In late August of 1991, the Ada Evening News reported, in depth, on the banner year that was expected from the Ada High School football team. The Oak Hills Country Club was preparing for their annual fund raising golf tournament that benefits Valley View Hospital. The Ada branch of the State Arts and Humanities Council began casting for the theater season at East Central University. A list of Ada's graduating seniors enrolled at the University of Oklahoma in Norman, Oklahoma and Oklahoma State University in Stillwater, Oklahoma for the fall semester appeared on the front page of the newspaper. A new restaurant opened in the south part of town and petitions for "liquor by the drink" were once again being circulated by the "wets", as this question would be on the ballot in the November election. George Herbert Walker Bush's approval rating was at 70%. The news of the Criminal Court of Appeal's decision to affirm the jury's verdict in the case of Dennis Fritz and Ronald Williamson was not mentioned.

Sometime before Christmas, a jogger discovered the body of Floyd Jones. The jogger was running on the country road by the Rosedale Cemetery where Debbie Carter was buried. Floyd apparently had been dead for several days. There had been snow a few days before the discovery was made, but a warm front melted the snow on the day the jogger discovered Floyd. An old bicycle lay in a ditch beside the body. The coroner stated that the deceased likely skidded off the road and suffered a concussion.

The breakfast crowd at the Parkview had changed over the past ten years. Several of the old timers had passed on and the younger customers were in a hurry. The city council approved an ordinance that required smoking and non-smoking sections in all restaurants. Some of these new customers began asking for things like yogurt and whole-wheat toast without butter.

"What is this world coming to?" Agnes asked the cook. "Folks are getting so worried about having a heart attack they can't even enjoy a good meal."

The cook shook his head.

"Just take poor old Floyd. He ate whatever he could find. Lived way past seventy and died from hitting his head on a rock."

"The world's moving mighty fast."

"I'll bet it ain't moving very fast for those two guys up at the State pen. I heard their appeals got turned down. How long has that Williamson boy been on death row now?'

"About six years now, but it may not be much longer for him."

"How do you know that?"

"I got a cousin up there at McAlester."

"In the penitentiary?"

"Yep."

"I didn't know you had a cousin."

"Well, Agnes, I don't tell everything I know."

"You may not tell everything you know, but every time I ask you to explain something to me that I don't understand, you always do. How'd you get to be so smart?"

"I'm not gonna tell you."

There are no windows in the cells on death row at the Oklahoma State prison in McAlester. Pictures are prohibited. The mattress rests on a cement slab that protrudes from the wall. Cement shelves hold a few personal items. Prisoners are locked down for twenty-three hours a day.

Because of Ron Williamson's deteriorating mental condition, he was not allowed to come in contact with any other prisoners in his one hour outside his cell in the 'yard'. Actually, the 'yard' was nothing more than a room located outside the cells that would hold only four or five men. When he went to this room, he went alone. Although Williamson was only forty years old, he looked seventy. His weight had dropped by more than fifty pounds. His hair, completely white, fell in strings over his gaunt face. Most of his teeth were missing due to cancer of the mouth that had not been treated. When he screamed his cries of innocence, his raspy voice was that of an old and desperate man. Often the guards would taunt him over the loudspeaker, speaking in high voices, saying, "Why did you kill me – kill me – kill me?"

His reply would come in anguished screams of innocence. "I didn't kill you Debbie Carter – I am an innocent man."

He had been without any kind of medication for more than seven years.

Those convicted of a crime are entitled to but one writ of error, or one appeal, or one review by certiorari. However, if a proceeding for review has been dismissed without a decision on the merits of a case, or abandoned, or when it is ineffectual so that it in no way brings up the merits of the case for review, and the time has not expired, another appeal may be prosecuted.

Failure of a defendant to follow appellate procedural rules subjects the defendant to dismissal. Generally, the accused does not have an absolute right to be present at proceedings in an appellate court.

In general, the appellate court in a criminal case may review only such matters as are within its power and authority to determine. The issue on the appeal is whether prejudicial error was committed against the accused.

The death sentence is subject to heightened scrutiny on appeal and will be reviewed to insure that it has not been applied in an arbitrary or capricious manner. While the scope of review in death penalty cases is broad, every decision to impose the death penalty implicates the procedural and substantive protections of the Eighth Amendment, and a review of such decisions by a state appellate court must, at a minimum, be sufficient to satisfy such protections.

Thus, Ron Williamson was afforded legal assistance after his appeal to the Criminal Court of Appeals was rejected, whereas Dennis Fritz was not.

Many times, Fritz, acting as his own attorney, requested that blood, semen and hair be examined for DNA evidence that he felt would prove his innocence. However, the State funds did not provide financing for these tests, saying that the State is not required to finance a fishing expedition for a defendant in the vain hope that 'something will turn up'.

Several people in the federal appellate public defender's office had been watching this case since the conviction in 1988. One of them, Kim Alyce Marks, an investigator in this office had researched testimony, files, court records and evidence since the Court of Criminal Appeals affirmed the decision of the state trial court in Pontotoc County as to the conviction of both Fritz and Williamson. Williamson's attorneys proceeded to assert his claims, first before the Oklahoma courts, as was required. His direct appeal was not decided by the Oklahoma Court of Criminal Appeals until 1991, and was not final until upon denial of the certiorari by the U.S. Supreme Court until April 1992. The Oklahoma Court's decision denying state post-conviction relief was not final on denial of certiorari until May 23, 1994. Thus, a request for a stay of execution and Williamson's habeas corpus petition were filed less than 120 days after the state process became final.

Ron Williamson's date for execution was scheduled for September 27, 1994, at 12:01 a.m.

In August 1994, Williamson's final appeal was denied. The day after this denial, a prison guard came to his cell and told him that the warden wanted to see him. Three guards escorted him to the Warden's office. The warden was sitting at a long table in his office. Williamson was told to sit at the end of this table facing the warden. Two guards stood on either side of Williamson as the warden said, "It is my duty to inform you that you have been sentenced to execution by lethal injection, and such sentence will be carried out at 12:01 a.m., September 24, 1994."

Williamson was then escorted to a holding cell near the death chamber that was double locked with two doors. These cells had more soundproofing, which muffled the screams of protest Ron Williamson shouted day and night.

His sister, Annette Hudson, was sent a form asking for the name of a funeral home where his body would be sent. The form also stated that he would be allowed no more than five visitors before his death.

CHAPTER EIGHTEEN

The Oklahoma Indigent Defense System's post-conviction attorneys logged over twelve hundred hours of overtime (hours over forty four per week) in the first six months of 1994. The vast majority of that overtime, and the overtime that continued to regularly accrue was entirely uncompensated.

Janet Chesley, the lead counsel had been responsible for a total of three extensive federal habeas corpus petitions in the months prior to the filing of the stay of execution of Williamson scheduled for September 27, 1994. In addition to her other substantial responsibilities, she personally worked innumerable late nights and weekends on this case.

The Emergency Application for a Stay of Execution and the following brief was filed in the U.S. District Court for the Eastern District of Oklahoma, on Thursday, September 22, 1994, less than five days (three working days) before Ron Williamson's execution by lethal injection.

EMERGENCY APPLICATION FOR STAY OF EXECUTION

PURSUANT TO 28 U.S.C. SECTIONS 2251 AND 1651
AND BRIEF IN SUPPORT

"This is Ronald Williamson's first appearance in federal court to pursue his constitutional habeas corpus remedies. Ronald Williamson will be put to death by lethal injection on Tuesday morning, September 27, 1994, at 12:01 a.m., unless this court grants this application for stay of execution.

Ronald Williamson is in the custody of the State of Oklahoma, pursuant to an unconstitutional conviction of first-degree murder and sentence of death imposed by the District Court of Pontotoc County Oklahoma. Mr. Williamson attacks the illegal conviction and sentence by Habeas corpus. Venue of the habeas corpus action, and the emergency stay request, is proper in the Eastern District of Oklahoma.

The procedural history of the case is set forth in detail in the habeas petition. In summary, Mr. Williamson has proceeded through the direct appeal and post-conviction process in the Oklahoma State courts. Those courts refused to apply the United States Constitution and grant him the relief to which he is entitled.

The Oklahoma post-conviction courts did not afford Mr. Williamson an evidentiary hearing, though his claims clearly present issues of fact. Consequently, a meaningful evidentiary hearing is mandatory in this court.

Because of constitutionally flawed proceedings, crucial information about this case and Mr. Williamson was unknown to the jurors who placed Ron Williamson in imminent peril of execution. Mr. Williamson is an individual who suffers from serious mental illness. His statement that he had a dream about committing the offense was accepted by law enforcement as a confession despite the fact that he denied committing the crime. Another individual, Rickey Joe Simmons, made a videotaped confession to the rape and murder but this was never made known to the jury. Also not before the jury were Mr. Williamson's videotaped statements denying any involvement in the offense. Also unknown to the jury was information regarding Mr. Williamson's mental health that would have explained his strange and inaccurate dream and would have been vital in mitigation. Indeed, no mitigation case whatever was presented on behalf of Mr. Williamson.

The shocking breakdowns of our judicial system outlined above occurred due to a combination of prosecutorial misconduct, failure of the state to provide funds for an adequate defense, and ineffectiveness of appointed counsel. They serve as but summary examples of some of the many substantial constitutional claims contained in the habeas corpus petition, all of which are incorporated here by reference.

Mr. Williamson has always maintained his innocence. There is every indication that he is, in fact, innocent. Certainly the proceedings that resulted in his conviction and sentence are so flawed that they cannot be relied upon to have produced a just result. Mr. Williamson looks to this court to enforce the constitution and safeguard his rights. Those ends cannot be accomplished by means of an expedited and meaningless process. They required the careful attention the federal courts accord to the most important cases that come before them.

As indicated, contemporaneously with the filing of this emergency stay application; Mr. Williamson has submitted an extensive habeas corpus petition pursuant to 28 U.S.C. & 2254. The petition attacks the validity of the judgment and death sentence on federal constitutional grounds, some of which are summarized above. Mr. Williamson's petition asks that this Court, acting as a guardian of the rights protected by the United States Constitution, carefully review and consider his claims and ultimately, grant him habeas corpus relief from his unconstitutional conviction and sentence. Because a habeas corpus petition is now on file with this Court, Ronald Williamson is entitled to a stay of execution pursuant to 28 U.S.C. &2251, pending a full and fair consideration of the issues by this Court.

This matter is of the utmost urgency. Ronald Williamson's execution is scheduled for 12:01 a.m., Tuesday, September 27, 1994. Less than three weekdays remain before the execution is to be carried out.

Mr. Williamson has proceeded diligently to assert his claims, first before the Oklahoma Courts, as he is required to do, and now before this federal forum as he has the right to do. His direct appeal was not decided by the Oklahoma Court of Criminal Appeals until 1991 and was not final upon denial of certiorari to the United States Supreme Court until April 1992. The Oklahoma Court's decision denying state post conviction relief was not final on denial of certiorari until May 23, 1994. Thus this request for a stay of execution and Mr. Williamson's habeas corpus petition are being filed less than 120 days after the state process became final.

Undersigned counsel has been assigned to Mr. Williamson's case. Due to extreme demands placed on the limited resources of OIDS, and particularly upon undersigned counsel, including essential work required in other cases with execution dates and other matters with firm filing deadlines, it was not possible to immediately direct attention to preparing a habeas corpus petition for Mr. Williamson. To have done so would have required ignoring even more urgent matters that needed to be prepared for other capital clients and thus would have substantially and permanently jeopardized their rights. On August 23, 1994, the Oklahoma Attorney General filed a notification with the Oklahoma Court of Criminal Appeals seeking an execution date for Mr. Williamson. Undersigned counsel did not receive notice of the setting of an execution date until Monday, August 29, 1994, a mere four weeks before the scheduled execution.

Upon information and belief, the purpose of obtaining an execution date was to promote a filing of a federal habeas corpus petition. The State of Oklahoma undoubtedly understands that Mr. Williamson is entitled to fully and fairly litigate this quasi-civil action in federal court.

Only through extraordinary efforts, not just of undersigned counsel but of every other lawyer in the division as well, has it been possible to prepare and present a habeas corpus petition prior to the execution date. These efforts have, without question, drawn attention away from other important matters.

Mr. Williamson's petition presents a number of complex and crucially important grounds for relief. Full and fair consideration of the petition will require discovery and an evidentiary hearing. Full and fair consideration is not possible in the short time remaining before the execution is to take place. Indeed, that would have been true even had it been possible to file the petition much earlier. A stay of execution should be entered so this court may give its careful attention to this case and so that counsel may assist the Court by fully developing the case."

In summary, the petition stated, "Ronald Williamson is proceeding in federal court. That is what the State desires that he do. The State no doubt recognizes that Ronald Williamson is entitled to a meaningful federal review of his claims.

Mr. Williamson is entitled to a stay of execution to allow him to properly present his claims to the federal courts. This Court has the jurisdiction and venue to hear Ronald Williamson's habeas Corpus petition but only if Ronald Williamson is alive to present his claim. The state must not execute Ronald Williamson before this Court has had a chance to meaningfully review his substantial federal claims.

This Court must, under the authority of the 28 U.S.C. &2251, grant a stay of execution to remain in effect until such time as Ronald Williamson's federal habeas proceedings are finally decided. Alternatively, this Court should grant a stay of execution pursuant to 28 U.S.C. & 1651 in order to preserve the jurisdiction of the federal courts.

In conclusion and prayer, Ronald Williamson respectfully asks this Court, for the reasons explained above, to issue a STAY OF EXECUTION prohibiting the State of Oklahoma from carrying out the judgment and sentence of death."
Respectfully submitted,
    Janet Chesley
    Appellate Defense Counsel

Oklahoma Indigent Defense System
Capital Post-Conviction Division
1660 Cross Center Drive
Norman, Oklahoma 73019
Attorney for Ronald Williamson
September 22, 1994

CERTIFICATE OF SERVICE

This is to certify that on the 22nd day of September 1994, I hand delivered a true and correct copy of this Emergency Application For a Sty of Execution pursuant to 28 U.S.C. #2251 and 1651 to:

Susan Brimer Loving
Attorney General for the State of Oklahoma
Diane Blalock
Assistant Attorney General
112 State Capitol Building
Oklahoma City, Oklahoma 73105

It was almost noon on September 22, when Janet Chesley delivered the emergency Application for a Stay of Execution to Susan Loving's office. The Attorney General was at lunch and her assistant on vacation. Janet waited for more than two hours before she could actually hand-deliver the application to the Attorney General. The secretary had offered to give the material to Ms. Loving when she returned to the office, but Janet and the others in the Indigent Defense office had worked too hard on this petition for Ron Williamson to take any chance of delay. Besides, the clock was ticking and the two hours Janet waited seemed to be much longer.

When Janet returned from the hand delivery, her co-counsel, Vicki Werneke, looked up from the stack of paper work on her desk and raised her eyebrows in anticipation of a report of the delivery.

"Done," Janet said.

Vicki raised her hand and crossed her fingers for luck.

CHAPTER NINETEEN

President Jimmy Carter appointed U.S. District Judge Frank H. Seay to the Court in 1979. Judge Seay, a native Oklahoman, born in Shawnee Oklahoma in 1938, received his BA from the University of Oklahoma in 1960 and his LLB from there in 1963. He practiced law in the community of Seminole, Oklahoma until 1966, when he became the Assistant District Attorney for the 22nd Judicial District of Oklahoma. He served in this position until 1968, when he was appointed as the District Judge of the 22nd Judicial District. This 22nd Judicial District includes both Seminole, where Judge Seay presided as well in Ada, Oklahoma where Judge Ronald Jones presided over the trial of Dennis Fritz and Ron Williamson.

In Oklahoma, there are three U.S. District Courts, the largest being the Western District located in Oklahoma City, the Northern District in Tulsa and the Eastern District in Muskogee. Judge Seay, in September 1994, was the only U.S. District judge in the Eastern District. He had been the only judge in this district since his appointment in 1979.

Judge Seay ran his court with a tight hand. The attorneys who practiced there never appeared without being prepared. Delays were unacceptable. Chief Judge Seay had little tolerance for criminals. No attorney had ever accused him of being 'soft on crime'.

Judge Seay followed the Fritz and Williamson trials closely. He knew the attorneys who had been appointed by the court for the defendants. He knew Barney Ward, the blind attorney who for many years, maintained a successful practice despite this serious handicap. Bill Peterson, the District Attorney who prosecuted the case, served with him on several committees when Judge Seay was in the District Attorney's office. However, even though he had not been in the courtroom during the trial, he remembered clearly the murder in 1982, the dream confession, and the mental instability of the man given the death penalty, which happened five years after the crime was committed. However, by the time the appeals were exhausted and Ron Williamson's execution date was set, Judge Seay had been on the federal court for more than fourteen years.

The application of the petitioner, Williamson, to proceed with supporting documentation with the order granting permission to proceed was entered on September 23, 1994.

The Petition for Writ of Habeas Corpus by the petitioner was entered that same day as was the Emergency Application for a Stay of Execution and Brief in Support.

The attorneys, Janet Chesley and Vicki Werneke, appeared in support of this submitted petition on September 23, 1994.
The Response by the respondent, Dan Reynolds, Warden, State Penitentiary at McAlester, Oklahoma, was also entered on that day. The Order by chief Judge Frank H. Seay granting a Stay of Execution was entered on September 26, 1994. This Order was faxed to the Attorney General of the State of Oklahoma, Susan Loving, Warden Dan Reynolds, the Tenth Circuit Court in Denver, Colorado, the United States Supreme Court and the Petitioner's counsel of record. This filing was complete less than eight hours before Ron Williamson's scheduled execution.

During the following year, Orders were filed and Responses made to these orders. On January 24, 1995, Judge Seay directed the respondents to make the trial transcripts and other pertinent state court files a part of the record and filed by February 7, 1995.

On February 10, 1995, an Order was entered directing the petitioner to submit, within seven days, (1) jury instructions for the first and second stages of petitioner's trials; (2) copies of the studies cited in the Brief of the Appellant in petitioner's appeal to the Oklahoma Court of Criminal Appeals, and (3) original photographs used as exhibits in petitioner's trial.

On June 7, 1995, Petitioner Ronald Williamson filed the Petition for Writ of Habeas Corpus in federal court.

After carefully reviewing all of the files and documents, on September 19, 1995, Judge Seay's order issued a Writ of Habeas Corpus, which granted Ronald Williamson a new trial, was filed in the U.S. District Court for the Eastern District of Oklahoma. The following statement prefaced his order:

"While considering my decision in this case I told a friend, a layman, I believed the facts and law dictated that I must grant a new trial to a defendant who had been convicted and sentenced to death. My friend asked, "Is he a murderer?"

I replied simply, "We won't know until he receives a fair trial. God help us, if ever in this great country we turn our heads while people who have not had fair trials are executed. That almost happened in this case."

ACCORDINGLY, the Writ of Habeas Corpus shall issue, unless within one hundred twenty (120) days of the entry of this Order the State grants Petitioner a new trial, or in the alternative, orders his permanent release from custody.

IT IS SO ORDERED this 19th day of September 1995.
Frank H. Seay
United States District Judge

In Summary, Judge Seay's Order granting a Writ of Habeas Corpus stated:

"The Petitioner, Ronald Williamson, was convicted of First Degree Murder and condemned to death in 1988, by the District Court of Pontotoc County, Oklahoma. On direct appeal, the Oklahoma Court of Criminal Appeals affirmed Williamson's conviction and death sentence. Williamson then filed an application for Post-Conviction Relief before the District Court of Pontotoc County, which was denied by that court on the 18th day of September 1992. The Oklahoma Court of Criminal Appeals affirmed the trial court's Denial of Post-Conviction Relief.

Williamson now seeks relief from his death sentence, asserting that his conviction and death sentence were obtained in violation of the Fifth, Sixth, Eighth and Fourteenth Amendments to the United States Constitution. Mr. Williamson has not previously sought habeas corpus relief in federal court.

On December 8, 1982, twenty-one year old Debra Sue Carter was found dead in her garage apartment in Ada, Oklahoma. The police were called, and the investigation into the murder began. Four years and five months later, on May 8, 1987, Ronald Williamson and Dennis Fritz were charged with the murder of Debbie Carter. Separate trials were held, and approximately two weeks before Williamson's trial began, Dennis Fritz was found guilty and sentenced to life imprisonment. Williamson was sentenced to death. Because Williamson's competency is the threshold issue, this court will first examine that claim.

1. COMPETENCY

Ineffective assistance of counsel claims may fall into two categories. First are the claims that the defendant was deprived of his right to effective assistance of counsel because counsel simply failed to provide adequate legal assistance. Second are the claims that the government violated the defendant's right to effective assistance of counsel by impermissibility interfering with counsel's ability to make independent decisions about how to conduct the defense.

To prove counsel's performance was deficient under an 'actual ineffectiveness' claim, Williamson must show that 'counsel's performance was deficient' with reference to prevailing professional norms and 'that the deficient performance prejudiced the defense'. Prejudice is shown by demonstrating 'there is a reasonable probability that, but for counsel's unprofessional error, the result of the proceeding would have been different'.

This review must be approached with considerable restraint. 'Judicial scrutiny of counsel's performance must be highly deferential. It is all too tempting for a defendant to second-guess counsel's assistance after conviction or adverse sentence, and it is all too easy for a court, examining counsel's defense after it has proved unsuccessful, to conclude that a particular act of omission of counsel was unreasonable.'

Williamson argues he was denied effective assistance of counsel during the first stage of trial by counsel's failure to fully investigate and utilize evidence of his mental illness.

Williamson has been observed and treated for mental illness since 1979. However, in spite of his lengthy incompetence in the same district court in an unrelated case two and one-half years earlier, his competency to stand trial in this case was never determined. Williamson's counsel was aware of some of these mental illness problems. Counsel's stated reason for not pursing this issue was that Williamson had already been found competent in 1985, in another criminal proceeding. This statement reveals that counsel's decision was based on both inadequate information and a decision was based on both inadequate information and a misconception of the law. On September 26, 1985, approximately three years before Williamson's trial in this case, a special district judge for the District Court of Pontotoc County, Oklahoma found Williamson mentally ill and unable to assist counsel. The judge in that case officially adjudged and decreed that Williamson was unable to appreciate the nature of the charges against him, consult with his counsel or rationally assist in his defense. Dr. Charles W. Amos recommended that Williamson be transferred to Eastern State Hospital for evaluation. This evaluation of Williamson's incompetence determination by Dr. Amos was available to counsel at the time of this trial, as was a letter from Ms. Norma Walker from the Mental

Health Services of Southern Oklahoma, who outlined the various times Williamson had utilized the services of that facility since 1980. In her affidavit she states that 'If I had been contacted by Mr. Williamson or his attorney, I would have been willing to assist and cooperate with Mr. Williamson's defense in the prosecution of murder charges against him in May of 1987.

These documents clearly indicate a problem that should have alerted counsel that further investigation was necessary before he made the critical decision either to proceed to trial or forego an insanity defense. Further, if counsel had visited with members of Williamson's family, he would have discovered that information contained in their affidavits attached to this order.

Ms. Walker's progress notes on December 20, 1986, state: 'Williamson's sister (Annette Hudson) called asking to see me with Ron and her husband, Marlin. Saw the three of them. Annette wanted to know what to do. Ron refused to go to the hospital voluntarily but was not psychotic enough to be committed. Sister reports talk of suicide by gun. He will probably be violent if an attempt is made to E.O.D. him

On November 9, 1987, after his incarceration for the murder of Debbie Carter, Ron Williamson was granted Disability Benefits due to mental disorder by the Department of Human Services of Oklahoma. These medical records were available to counsel at the time of trial'.

The following statements and opinions of counsel are set forth in counsel's own affidavit:

"At virtually every appearance there was some kind of outburst from Mr. Williamson. At the preliminary hearing he became so incensed that he turned a table over on my secretary and the counsel for Dennis Fritz. At that point he had to be removed from the courtroom. The judge gave Mr. Williamson more than one opportunity to return to the proceeding, but he always refused. As a result he missed the entire preliminary hearing.

At the jury trial he continued to be disruptive. He argued with the prosecutor and the witnesses in front of the jury, and made a poor argumentative witness. Because of my previous experience with Mr. Williamson, I had expected some trouble, and consequently I arranged to have my son sit behind me during the trial with instruction to bring him to the ground if he made any sudden move toward me. On the whole I found my representation of Mr.

Williamson to be an extremely unpleasant experience and I was glad to get this case over with.

I was aware that Mr. Williamson was receiving medication in the Pontotoc County Jail, and was receiving medicine through Dr. Marie Snow, a local psychiatrist associated with Mental health Services of Oklahoma. On occasion the jailers would call me when Mr. Williamson ran out of medication and I would contact the personnel at Mental Health Services to arrange for Dr. Snow to call in another prescription. The only name of the drugs prescribed for Mr. Williamson at that time that I can remember is Thorazine. Early on in my representation of Mr. Williamson I became concerned that he was being over medicated because he appeared to be too drowsy on occasions when I would attempt to interview him. As a result of this problem, I requested that his dosage be reduced. Dr. Snow is an elderly lady, and is the only psychiatrist in Ada. I did not find her to be very communicative regarding Mr. Williamson's mental condition. I never had a formal interview with her regarding Williamson, nor did I subpoena her for the trial or any hearing. However, on one occasion she told me not to let the jailers lock me in the cell with Mr. Williamson.

I want the record to show that I am now making application to withdraw. That boy won't cooperate with me at all. If he was paying me, I wouldn't be here. I can't represent him, judge. Can't do it. I don't know who's going to, but I can't, and if I can't get relief here, I'm going to see if I can't get it from the Court of Criminal… I'm not going to put up with this. I'm too damn old for it. I don't want anything to do with him, not under any circumstances."

It appears that Williamson's conduct became so outrageous during the preliminary hearing that counsel inquired of the judge, "Do you want me to load him down with about a hundred milligrams of-------------?"

Ronald Williamson was arrested on a Friday night. He was taken from his cell within twenty-four hours of his arrest to be interrogated by Agents Featherstone and Rogers of the OSBI. Petitioner had been interviewed at least twice previously regarding this homicide and had steadfastly denied any involvement. Agent Rogers testified that Williamson verbally waived his Miranda rights and proceeded to relate that he had a dream about killing the victim. Agent Rogers also testified that the interview was terminated when Williamson invoked his right to counsel.

After this purported confession had already been presented to the jury, the trial court held a hearing to determine its voluntariness. During the hearing, Agent Rogers testified that Williamson appeared to understand his actions, and he was neither influenced by alcohol or drugs nor threatened or coerced. On cross-examination, Agent Featherstone testified that, "Williamson was not calm, cool and collected, yet we could understand what he was saying." Counsel failed to explore this statement to discover the cause of Williamson's agitation. Agent Rogers admitted he did not videotape, audiotape, write or read the purported confession for Williamson's review or signature, although equipment to properly record Williamson's statement was readily available.

Counsel filed no motions challenging the admissibility of the admissions or the confession based on voluntariness due to the manner in which they were secured or the apparent mental problems of Williamson. Further, counsel presented no evidence at the hearing concerning the lack of a knowing and intelligent waiver by Williamson of his Miranda rights, although Williamson's admissions and confession were made during a period in 1987 when he had been in and out of mental institutions and on and off medication.

Williamson's mental illness may have rendered it impossible for him to understand his constitutional rights, or to waive them knowingly, intelligently, or voluntarily. Any use of any involuntary confession against a defendant in a criminal trial violates due process. The most important point not investigated by counsel was the fact that Williamson was not on his medication when he waived his rights and gave the dream confession. In fact, he had been off his medication for over a month and remained un-medicated until June 1987. Thus, Agent Rogers and Featherstone questioned Williamson during a time when he may have been suffering from delusional thoughts, impaired consciousness and confused thinking.

In the penalty stage of the trial, counsel failed to produce any mitigating evidence. In Oklahoma, the jury is required to weigh the aggravating and mitigating factors to determine whether the death penalty should be imposed. In this case, the jury found that the following three aggravating factors applied to the murder: (1) there exists a probability that the defendant would commit criminal acts of violence that would constitute a continuing threat to society, (2) the murder was especially heinous, atrocious or cruel, and (3) the murder was committed for the purpose of avoiding or preventing a lawful arrest or prosecution. Counsel rested at the conclusion of the State's case and presented no mitigating evidence favorable to the defendant. Had trial counsel investigated and secured the necessary witnesses, he could have presented evidence of Williamson's life history, his increasing inability to function and the considerable medical documentation.

Given the weakness of the case against Williamson, this court had little doubt that the available mitigating evidence would have changed the jury's decision to impose the death penalty. Williamson contends counsel was ineffective for failing to adequately investigate two witnesses and for failing to utilize certain evidence concerning these witnesses.

Counsel did not thoroughly investigate and present evidence concerning Glen Gore as a suspect in this case. Glen Gore was admittedly the last person to see Debra Sue Carter alive. Tommy Glover testified for the prosecution that he saw Gore talking to Ms. Carter as she was getting into her car to leave the club, although Glover's testimony at trial made this discussion in the parking lot seem innocuous, persons who worked with Glover have stated that as Glover related the incident at the time – in December, 1982 – Gore and Ms. Carter were arguing and Gore shoved her into the car. This information was not relayed to Williamson's trial counsel until after the jury had reached its verdict in the guilt phase of the trial.

Gore agreed to submit to a polygraph examination, but one was never administered. He said he gave hair samples at least twice, but when these samples were finally examined in 1988, the OSBI failed to compare them to the 32 unidentified hairs found in the victim's apartment. Rather, the State's expert inexplicably compared the Gore hairs to the slides he was preparing to testify about in court, which were hair already identified as consistent with Debra Carter, Williamson and Fritz. Finally, although fingerprints for 23 suspects and 21 other individuals who had been in the victim's apartment were sent to the OSBI for comparison with the prints found in the apartment; Gore's fingerprints were never submitted.

At the time Gore stated he would not testify at Williamson's trial, he was serving a forty-year sentence on charges of burglary, kidnapping, shooting with intent to kill, feloniously pointing a weapon. However, a plea bargain agreement was entered just one week after Gore was listed as an additional witness and the prosecution then dropped a second kidnapping charge and a charge of assault and battery with a dangerous weapon. Also, the letter from the parents of the young woman who feared for her life and the life of her child – filed on June 3, 1987 – was available to counsel, but counsel failed to investigate any of Gore's prior convictions. As a result, the jury never knew about Gore's offenses that involved an assault on a woman and her child, that he had previously attacked this same woman on numerous occasions, and that he had entered into a plea bargain with the district attorney just one week after being listed as an additional witness in this case. Also, if counsel had interviewed Tommy Glover, he might have learned that Glover originally related to co-workers that the "conversation" he saw Gore having with Carter in the Coachlight parking lot was actually an argument and that Gore had shoved Ms. Carter at the end of their encounter.

Counsel also accepted the testimony of the State's hair expert, Melvin Hett, that Hett had compared Gore's hair samples to the unidentified hairs found in the victim's apartment. Although the State contributed to this failure by not turning over Hett's report until he was actually testifying, counsel ultimately missed the fact that the report could not eliminate Gore as a suspect. As a result, the prosecutor was able to argue in closing that Gore had been "eliminated", when, in fact, he had not.

Another troubling aspect of this case concerned the motivation of one of the State's most important witnesses, Terri Holland, in prison on three felony charges. Her testimony provided the only evidence of straightforward admission of guilt by Williamson. Those felony charges were reduced after her testimony. This court found that counsel was ineffective for failing to bring Terri Holland's background to the attention of the jury.

In September of 1987, while Williamson was being held in the Pontotoc County Jail, Rickey Joe Simmons voluntarily came into the Ada Police Station to confess to the murder of Debbie Carter. The investigator videotaped the interview and repeatedly tried to convince Simmons he had not killed Ms. Carter, but was instead mentally ill. Counsel had access to this videotape long before trial, yet he did not attempt to introduce the tape or reveal the existence of the Simmons confession during the trial. The jury was never informed that Simmons had told police that he raped and killed Debra Carter.

Counsel stated that he could not remember why he did not bring this evidence to the attention of the jury, which indicates that this omission was not the result of a rational trial strategy. Counsel said, "Upon reflection, I think that I should have attempted to do so because Simmons confession was as believable as was Mr. Williamson's."

Had counsel used the evidence available to him, the jury would have gone into deliberation with the knowledge that two men, both with apparent mental problems had given factually inaccurate confessions to the same crime."

This court added the following statement at the end of this part of the opinion regarding the competency of defense counsel. "Although defense counsel was legally ineffective in Williamson's trial, this Court is well aware of his many years of credible service to the public in both criminal and civil matters. Williamson's case points out the critical need for public defenders that are specialists in criminal death penalty defense. Quality representation of indigent defendants requires adequate funding which allows reasonable limits on attorney's caseloads and effective support resources. The system in which private attorneys are appointed to these cases is afflicted with many pitfalls, including inexperience, unmanageable caseloads and meager compensation for services."

The prosecution's only physical evidence, apart from semen evidence, were hairs allegedly found to be "microscopically consistent" with Williamson and his co-defendant, Dennis Fritz. Dennis Smith, retried detective captain of the Ada Police Department, testified that he and OSBI Agent Gary Rogers collected several hundred hairs at the crime scene. However, about a year and a half after the murder, Smith could not remember whether Glen Gore's hair samples had been submitted.

Modern hair experts generally state their results in testimony that samples are "similar" and "could have" come from the "same source". Critics of hair evidence have criticized the admission of hair evidence on the grounds that it is too subjective and it has a high error rate.

This court, therefore, finds that the introduction into evidence of expert hair testimony at Williamson's trial was irrelevant, imprecise and speculative and its probative value was outweighed by its prejudicial effect.

CHAPTER TWENTY

It had been a hot summer, with little rain and by October of 1995, the temperatures still hovered in the nineties. The Wednesday night prayer meeting at the First Baptist Church directed its supplications for moisture to the divine powers. The governor determined that a cloud seeding program would be investigated if the drought continued.

"Hot." The old man fanned himself with his ball cap as he sipped his coffee at the Parkview Café.

"The coffee or the weather?" the younger man asked.

"Both."

"This newspaper here says that the governor is praying for rain."

"That's something I'd like to see."

"What? The governor praying for rain?"

"The governor praying."

"Something else here – way back on the last page."

"Yeah?"

"Looks like Ron Williamson might be getting a new trial."

"Who?"

"Williamson – that boy who got the death penalty back in '88 for murdering that Carter girl."

"I remember. Almost got executed didn't he."

"Would have, too, if that federal judge up there in Muskogee hadn't stopped it."

"Why'd he stop it?"

"Didn't get a fair trial."

"What was wrong with the trial?"

"Well, for one thing, the boy was documented crazy."

"Oh, hell, everybody knew that. Personally I think we needed to get him off the street. I heard he was a window peeper."

"Good God, man, you don't send a man to the death chamber for window peeping."

"A new trial you say."

The Tenth Circuit Court of Appeals received Judge Seay's Order granting a new trial for Ron Williamson on October 1, 1995.

The Circuit Court usually takes up to eighteen months to review the opinion of the U.S District Court and issue a ruling.

On April 10, 1997, some seventeen months after receiving this Order from Judge Seay, the Circuit Court filed a thirty-seven page Brief affirming the District Court's Order which conclusion follows:

"In conclusion, we hold that counsel was constitutionally inadequate in failing to fully investigate Mr. Williamson's history of mental illness, failing to seek a competency determination, failing to challenge the credibility of his client's confession, and failing to investigate and present to the jury the fact that another man had confessed to the crime. Because Mr. Williamson was prejudiced by counsel's ineffectiveness, he is entitled to relief. Accordingly, we AFFIRM the ruling of the district court directing that Mr. Williamson be granted a new trial within 120 days or permanently released from custody."

On June 10, 1997, the State District Court of Pontotoc County ordered that Ron Williamson be returned to the prison in McAlester from the State Hospital where he was under treatment for mental problems. However, this order was withdrawn as a result of a competency hearing in August, which found the defendant Williamson to be incompetent to undergo further criminal proceedings at this time.

Dr. Curtis Grundy stated that Williamson was a mentally ill person whose incompetence may be corrected within a reasonable period of time if he is provided a course of treatment, therapy and training. "If," Dr. Grundy said, "he were released without such treatment, he would pose a significant threat to the life and safety of himself and others."

The court then ordered Williamson be held in Maximum security at Eastern State Hospital for treatment and required that the Department of Mental Health provide a progress report every 60 days. On August 28, 1997, Dennis Fritz made an official request to the Pontotoc county Court that the Innocence Project of New York, be designated as a party representative who should be notified as to any concern regarding the DNA testing on the crime scene samples that were retrieved in the Debra Carter murder case.

Fritz had exhausted all his appeals through the courts, but he knew that when Williamson finally got a new trial, the DNA tests, which for years he had lobbied, would free both of them.

CHAPTER TWENTY-ONE

In 1989, a receptionist at a beauty salon and the mother of two girls, ages three and six, was taken from her home and raped in a wooded area nearby. She was unable to give the police a good description of the man. No other reports of assaults were documented in the area, but for years, she lived in fear that this man might someday return and attack her or her daughters.

In 1998, her husband, a police officer, told her about a man who had been arrested and charged with the rape of two other women. When his DNA was entered into the State's data bank, something now required by law in all but three states, it matched a semen sample recovered by the police in his wife's 1989 case.

The next step was to link the State's databases to a national system. This was happening rapidly. Not only was DNA a powerful tool in exonerating people of crimes they were accused of committing years ago, it made it possible to track down criminals who may have gone free.

In 1993, an American biochemist, Kary Mullis, won the Nobel Prize for Chemistry for his invention of the polymerase chain reaction (PCR), which was a simple technique that allows a specific stretch of DNA to be copied billions of times in a few hours.

At the time, this discovery was dramatic because of its applications for pharmaceutical and biomedical purposes, however the revolution it would create in courtrooms across the world were yet to be realized.

In the late 1980's, two biochemists, Henry Ehrlich and Edward Blake, discovered that the Mullis discovery could be used in criminal investigations. The same genetic material is found in every cell in the human body, but to remove this material, the cell wall must be opened to allow the DNA to escape.

Most cells are easy to open, but the walls of the sperm cells are tougher and thicker. In a sexual assault, two types of cells are collected with swabs – sperm cells from the rapist and skin cells from the victim. A mild cleaning solution will break open cells from the victim. A mild cleaning solution w``ill break open the victim's skin cells permitting the victim's DNA to be extracted, leaving behind the sperm cells from the rapist. It makes no difference whether this swab is tested immediately or whether it is tested years later. The victim's cells in the mix tell the investigators that they are looking in the right place for the rapist.

The DNA in a cell is contained in a small region called the nucleus. Although red blood cells do not contain nuclei, white cells do, so blood is easily typed for DNA. The cells in the outside layer of skin contain few or no nuclei, thus it makes it difficult or impossible to contaminate an object by casual handling. In order to type hair, it is generally necessary to obtain samples that include a root. Nail clippings, hair shafts and body fluids, such as urine, feces and perspiration, may or may not contain enough nucleated cells for DNA analysis. However, most internal organs, as well as bone, may be analyzed using DNA.

The amount of a sample needed to obtain a conclusive result varies, but less semen than blood is needed to obtain a conclusive result. This is because the concentration of sperm cells in semen is higher than the white cells in blood.

On November 25, 1997, the District Court of Pontotoc County was preparing for Ron Williamson's new trial. The preliminary hearing was scheduled for December 10, 1997, and Dr. Curtis Grundy, Williamson's psychiatrist at Eastern State Hospital, was ordered to report on the competency evaluation at that time. Dr. Grundy's report stated that Ron Williamson was a person incompetent to undergo further criminal proceedings at this time. Dr. Grundy's letter to the court read in part:

"During my evaluation of Mr. Williamson, he appeared agitated. He talked in a very loud manner and frequently utilized expletives. His speech was somewhat pressured. He answered most questions with responses regarding his thoughts and beliefs about 'Mr. Ricky Joe Simmons'. It became apparent that there were problems with his mental status which warranted further treatment."

In January, 1998, Dr. Grundy's letter to Judge Landrith regarding Williamson's mental condition stated:

" I have interviewed Mr. Williamson on several occasions since his return to the hospital. In general, his symptomatology appears to be exacerbated. His speech is pressured and loud. It appears that he has developed psychotic symptoms, evidenced by delusions of grandiosity and ideas of reference. For example, he recently informed me that a television reporter was going to assist in broadcasting information about his case throughout the world. He spoke as if he knew this television reporter, alluding to the belief that his special status of importance would allow him beneficial treatment from the media."

The old man sat at the table by the window of the Parkview, his younger friend across from him. They watched snow cover the windshields of the cars and trucks parked by the side of the building. Agnes poured hot coffee into their half filled cups.

"This cold weather makes my bones ache," the old man said. "I'll be damn happy to see spring come this year."

"How many springs have you seen?"

"If I live to see this one, it'll be seventy."

"Guess you've see a lot of changes here in Ada in seventy years."

"To tell the truth, Ada's pretty much the same as it was when I was a boy. Folks here don't like change much."

The young man reached for the sugar and stirred some into his cup. "I was in the barber shop yesterday. The talk is that the Williamson boy's new trial is coming up pretty soon."

"I've heard that."

"Not many folks like the idea of letting him out. I think they still believe he killed that girl no matter what happened at the trial or what all those new kind of tests show."

"Folks don't like to admit they made a mistake."

"Seems to me Bill Peterson's biggest nightmare has to be having to try that case again."

"You got that right."

They pushed back their chairs, stood and reached into pockets for change to leave for Agnes. "Much obliged." The old man smiled in her direction.

After the door closed, she cleared the table and pocketed the change. The place was empty except for her and the cook.

"Those boys wasn't guilty of nothing was they?"

"Nope," the cook answered.

"Did you know that all this time?"

"Suspected it."

"They been in there almost twelve years now."

"Nothing moves very fast in the justice system. I heard some rumors going around up there in the pen."

"From your cousin?"

The cook nodded. "Rumor is that Williamson told his doc up there at the hospital that a television reporter plans to interview him on national TV – put his story all over the country – maybe even put him in the movies."

"That'll be the day," Agnes said.

Meanwhile, Dennis Fritz filed a Motion for the Production of Physical Evidence for Inspection and Testing in the Pontotoc County Court on January 22, 1998.

He requested that DNA testing be done on the vaginal smears that were prepared and dry mounted upon slides by the OSBI Laboratories during the pendency of the past trial.

Also. The fabric cut from the torn blue panties containing semen stains, and one fitted sheet cut out of seminal stain should be first inspected by this lab site.

Judge Landrith, on November 30, 1998, ordered that fundamental fairness required that Fritz's motion be granted and that the defense expert from the Innocence Project be present at the time of DNA extraction.

On February 3, 1999, the Motion to Dismiss was filed in the District Court of Pontotoc County:

"The defense moves that the charges against Ron Williamson be dismissed. The defense moves that Ron Williamson be ordered released from custody immediately."

The defense stated:
- DNA testing has shown that neither Ron Williamson nor the co-defendant, Dennis Fritz, committed the sexual assault on Debra Sue Carter:
- In particular, at Lab Corporation of America in North Carolina, DNA was extracted from the panties of the victim and from the vaginal swab of the victim. Lab Corporation, chosen by the prosecution to act on behalf of the prosecution in DNA testing, has determined that the DNA does not belong to the victim, does not belong to Dennis Fritz, and does not belong to Ron Williamson.
- Forceful and damaging sexual assault occurred concurrently with the homicide and as part of the homicide by Debra Carter.

- The evidence now demonstrates that Ron Williamson and Dennis Fritz were not responsible for that brutal assault. They are innocent.

Because of these facts, it would be inappropriate to continue the prosecution and incarceration of Ron Williamson. More than that, it would be compounding a horrific miscarriage of justice if the charges against Mr. Williamson were not immediately dismissed and if Mr. Williamson were not immediately freed.

For a criminal defendant to be held for trial, "the evidence must coincide with guilt and be inconsistent with innocence." Considering the DNA results, the evidence and the alleged guilt of Mr. Williamson have collided rather than coincided. The case, which already has been derailed in terms of the evidence, should be derailed officially by the Court so that justice may be done.

Put simply, Ron Williamson is innocent and should be set free.

Although the court agreed with the DNA evidence regarding semen samples, it ruled that the hair samples be retested and that any documents pertaining to testing done by the Lab Corporation of America be sealed.

"The attorneys and parties shall not disclose to the public or persons not involved in the litigation, any suspect or suspects name or identity in any manner."

His attorney, Barry Sheck, filed a similar Motion to Dismiss in the case of Dennis Fritz on February, 1999.

CHAPTER TWENTY-TWO

Mark Barrett, Ron Williamson's attorney with the Indigent Defense System, had a long list of witnesses to interview as he began preparation for a possible new trial for his client.

Terri Holland, James Harjo, Mike Tinney, Dennis Smith, Gary Rogers and, of course, Glen Gore who was serving time – a forty year sentence for assault with a deadly weapon, kidnapping and burglary. Glen Gore topped his list and not just because Barrett knew where he could be located.

Barrett had been advised by Barry Sheck, the attorney representing Dennis Fritz, to bring along a swab. "What for?" Barrett had asked.

"Maybe he'll give you a DNA sample."

On February 12, 1999, Agnes opened the Parkview at 6:00 a.m. It was almost seven o'clock before the cook appeared at the front door, hurriedly tied the apron his waist and turned on the grille.

"Where've you been?" Agnes asked.

"Tell you later," he said as he put the bacon on the hot grille.

It was a busy Monday morning. The weather, cool and brisk, brought out the customers. It was almost eleven o'clock before the crowd cleared enough for Agnes to sit at the counter and visit with the cook through the pass-through window to the kitchen.

"Well, now tell me what's up. You got some woman moved in with you?"

"I was up at McAlester yesterday."

"Visiting your cousin?"

The cook nodded.

"And?"

"Remember that fellow – name's Glen Gore – who testified against Ron Williamson?"

"I remember."

"He had a visitor a couple of days ago – over at Lexington."

"Lexington's where the trustees stay."

"Right. They get a lot of privileges there. Gore gets to go over to a work site – ride a tractor and mow pastures – stuff like that."

"Who was his visitor?"

"Williamson's lawyer. My cousin said the word is out that this lawyer asked him about being the last person to see the Carter girl – shoving her in her car. Asked him about the plea bargain that got his sentence reduced from a hundred and twenty years down to forty."

"What's a plea bargain?"

"It's a deal you make with the prosecutor. If you agree to testify against somebody, he reduces your sentence."

"Why didn't your cousin do that?"

"He did. That's why he knows so much about it."

"Does that happen often?"

"Happens all the time."

"Whatever is this world coming to?"

"Another thing – this lawyer tried to get Gore to give him a saliva sample."

"How do you do that?"

"You take a Q-tip and swab your mouth with it. They can get a DNA sample that way."

"Now that's something I don't understand. What is it with this DNA test?"

"To tell the truth, all I know is they can test saliva and find out if you committed the crime. But Gore took that Q-tip and started to clean his ears with it. Then he broke it in half and put it in his pocket. He told that lawyer that if he wanted to see him again, he'd have to come over where he worked on the tractor."

"I don't think I'd do that!"

"My cousin said he wouldn't either."

Even though Judge Landrith had sealed the evidence that exonerated defendants Williamson and Fritz, the residents were speculating about their release – when it would be – how the police would handle it. Many of them remembered Williamson as a threat to their safety. They remembered the wild, crazy boy who played professional baseball for a time – who had trouble with the law and women. For twelve years, none of these citizens had seen him, but if they had, they would never have recognized him. This wild and foolish boy had been beaten down by the prison system. His hair was white, his cheeks sunken and his crooked smile revealed broken and missing teeth. Although in his mid-forties, he looked twenty years older. He was hardly the threat his neighbors feared.

On April 7, counsel for both defendants filed motions asking the court to vacate its order prohibiting information regarding the new suspect in the murder.

The State's database collected DNA samples from every convicted prisoner. Glen Gore's DNA was in this database and his DNA matched the semen found in Debbie Carter's vagina, anus and on her underwear.

Counsel's grounds for this motion were to make the court aware of death threats on the lives of both defendants. They felt that the public's fears would be lessened if they were made aware that Gore's DNA matched the physical evidence at the crime scene, thus making him the new suspect in the Carter case.

In the April 11, 1999, issue of the Ada Evening News, the headline read: HAIR SAMPLES DON'T MATCH. Marcia Eisenberg, director of the DNA testing portion of Lab Core, reportedly concluded the hairs taken from the crime scene are in no way consistent with Fritz or Williamson's DNA makeup.

District Attorney Peterson said, "At this point we don't know who the hairs belong to. We haven't tested them against anybody except Williamson and Fritz. There was no question in my mind when we started this whole DNA process that these two men were guilty. I wanted it (physical evidence) sent off for the purpose of getting these two guys. When we got the results on the semen samples, I was so surprised my jaw dropped to the floor."

Judge Landrith issued a gag order on information pertaining to another man, whose DNA profile reportedly matched the semen samples taken at the crime scene. The name of that man is not being released, the article said.

Barrett reported in this article that his client Williamson was happy when he heard the news about the test result on the hair, but didn't seem surprised.

"He spent more time talking about what he wanted to do when he got to Ada," Barrett said. "He misses things like cheeseburgers. Who knows what he'll want to do first when he's released. He and his family have talked about taking a vacation."

Barrett added that if Williamson is released on Thursday, April 14, he would not stay in Ada more than a few days before moving out of state.

When Peterson was asked what happens after the defendants are released, he said, "It's real simple. The case is reopened."

On Tuesday, April 13, 1999, Dennis Fritz was transported from the Dick Conners Correctional Center in Hominy, to the Pontotoc County Jail in Ada.

"It's the small things that really count for me now," he said when interviewed by the reporter from the Ada Evening News. "If nothing else comes from this whole experience, at least I have gained that perspective. I don't take anything for granted."

Fritz plans to return to Kansas City, Missouri when he is set free on Thursday.

"This case should never have been prosecuted," Fritz said. "The evidence they had against me was insufficient and if the police had done an adequate investigation of all the suspects this would never had happened."

He added that the way the indigent defense system was set up in 1987, also contributed to his conviction. "DNA testing should have been made available to use then, but the State wouldn't pay for it. When a person doesn't have the money to defend himself, he's at the mercy of the judicial system.

I don't blame my court appointed lawyer. He did the best job he could under the circumstances, but he practiced civil law, not criminal law.

There will always be people in this community, who don't believe that I'm innocent, and they are entitled to their opinion, but I know that I am innocent.

More important than my release from prison, " Fritz added, "is that the killer of Debbie Carter be found and convicted. All the time I was in prison, I wanted to get out, but much more, I wanted the truth to be brought to light. What was really important was the truth. I didn't want to be out walking around with this hanging over my head."

Ron Williamson was also transported to the Pontotoc County Jail on April 13, 1999 from Eastern State Hospital, accompanied by his psychiatrist, Dr. Kenneth Foster. Williamson's attorney entered a motion that permitted Williamson to continue his treatment under Dr. Foster's care. The court granted this request that same day.

On April 14, 1999, a crew from DATELINE appeared at the work site where Glen Gore worked. He had been cutting grass along the highway near the town of Purcell. The yard boss told them Gore was 'brush hogging' somewhere in the area and would be back in an hour or so for his lunch. When the reporters returned, Gore had not come in for lunch.

The reporters waited through the early part of the afternoon while the yard boss and his crew searched for Gore. "Gone," the boss told them. "Probably knew he was the suspect the newspaper wrote about yesterday."

"Was his name mentioned in the article?" the reporter asked.

"Didn't need to," the boss answered. "Most folks suspected him anyway."

"Can't believe he just disappeared," the reporter said.

"Not hard for him to disappear," the boss said, "he knows this country pretty good."

That afternoon, the lawyers, the judge and the prosecutor visited at the courthouse. Williamson and Fritz would be released the next morning. The conversation was friendly and relaxed. They remembered Williamson's days as an outstanding baseball player – his draft into the major leagues and his brushes with the law after his career ended.

Later in the afternoon when the news of Gore's disappearance reached the courthouse, Scheck and Barrett went across the street to the County Jail where Williamson and Fritz were chatting for the first time in twelve years.

They were dressed in black and white striped jailhouse pajamas. Williamson, six feet two, gaunt and white haired, smiled broadly, his bout with mouth cancer had taken all but a few of his teeth that were yellow with neglect.

Age and trouble had taken its toll on Fritz as well. His neatly trimmed hair, too, was graying. He was five feet eight inches tall and weighed about 150 pounds.

"I can hardly wait until its dark tomorrow night," Williamson said.

"Why's that" Barrett asked.

"I haven't seen the moon and stars for twelve years," he said. "Haven't walked through new grass barefoot or felt rain on my face."

"Haven't seen a Christmas tree," Fritz added, "or smelled pine branches after a spring shower."

"Got something to tell you boys," Barrett said. "Remember that guy who testified against you at your preliminary hearing?" he asked Williamson.

"You mean Gore?" Williamson frowned.

Barrett nodded. "He's gone."

"He ran?" Fritz asked.

"Some reporters came over to his work-release place to interview him and he left."

"Ran." Fritz repeated.

Williamson laughed out loud. "Damn," he said, "if he wasn't guilty he wouldn't have run."

"Here we are," Fritz said, "for two months we've known we were getting released because we were innocent and we were sitting in a high security prison, and he's got an outdoor job with privileges."

"And he runs," Williamson added.

At the jail the next morning, Williamson and Fritz dressed for court. Williamson wore a dark suit, white shirt, a yellow tie and an obviously new pair of blue and white athletic shoes.

Fritz wore gray slacks and a blue and white striped shirt. His reading glasses were in the breast pocket. Both men were hand cuffed as they walked separately across the lawn from the jail to the courthouse.

They were followed by dozens of cameramen, and radio broadcasters with microphones asking questions of them as they walked toward freedom.

"How are you feeling this morning?" one newscaster asked Williamson, following closely – microphone near so as not to miss a word.

"I'm feeling just fine this morning," he answered. "And how are you feeling this morning?" He smiled for the camera.

Ron Williamson's prediction to his psychiatrist Dr. Grundy was coming true. The story of his life was being played out on television the morning of April 15, 1999. And this day was only the beginning.

CHAPTER TWENTY-THREE

Judge Tom Landrith expected an overflow crowd in the small Ada courtroom the morning of April 15, 1999, but the assembled gathering far exceeded his expectations. Not only was the courtroom packed, people stood in the hallway and the yard was shoulder to shoulder. The day was beautiful with flowers blooming along the walks and the trees leafed out in new growth.

Judge Landrith's order, filed that morning, stated:
IT IS THEREFORE ORDERED, ADJUDGED AND DECREED that the Motions to Dismiss as to Defendants, Ronald Keith Williamson and Dennis Leon Fritz, be granted, and this action be dismissed without prejudice.
IT IS FURTHER ORDERED, ADJUDGED AND DECREED by the Court that the Defendant Ronald Keith Williamson, should be released instanter from incarceration with the Department of Corrections or Eastern State Hospital, and custody of the Pontotoc County Sheriff. That said release shall be only into the custody of Annette Hudson, Guardian of the Person and Estate of Ronald Keith Williamson.
IT IS FURTHER ORDERED, ADJUDGED AND DECREED by the Court that the Defendant, Dennis Leon Fritz, should be released instanter from incarceration with the Department of Corrections and custody of the Pontotoc County Sheriff.
Thomas Landreith
Judge

As the defendants stood before the Judge, Bill Peterson, the District Attorney, made the following statement: "It is my moral, ethical and legal duty to ask that this case be dismissed."

Judge Landrith said, "We cannot replace the twelve years these defendants have been incarcerated, nor can we forget Debra Carter. All we can do is move forward. What this day is, is a day of freedom."

"Gentlemen," Judge Landrith raised his gavel and looked at the two standing defendants, "you are free to go."

Williamson's attorney, Mark Barrett, called it "a day of celebration." Three other former Oklahoma prison inmates – one of whom had spent six of his years in prison on death row, flanked

Barrett and the two exonerated men. All were wrongfully convicted and imprisoned, but set free after many years because of new DNA comparison techniques.

"It's a great system we have. But we have to make it better. It is ruled too much by money, class and race," Barry Scheck added, and reminded that his Innocence Project based at New York University's Cardozo Law School, reviews hundreds of cases of wrongful imprisonment each year.

"God bless Barry Scheck," Fritz said. "I wouldn't say I'm angry at this point. But I've been angry – very bitter. I've tried to overcome those feelings and I plan to do everything I can to prevent this from happening to someone else."

Fritz was flanked by his mother and his daughter, Elizabeth, a beautiful elegantly dressed young woman of twenty-five. Although he had not seen her since she was thirteen, he had talked to her every day of the past twelve years. He knew about her friends, her schools, her career as manager of one of the leading telecommunication companies in the world. "I just can't wait to start our new life together." Elizabeth smiled and her smile was dazzling. "I finally have a family again."

When asked about Glen Gore as the new suspect in the case, Fritz said, "That makes everything total. It's the icing on the cake. I've wanted total exoneration from this charge. It's an unbelievable feeling. Unbelievable."

Williamson's sister, Annette Hudson, told reporters, "The joy is unspeakable. We knew he was innocent. We've been waiting for twelve years."

"At one point," Williamson said, "I had a little bit of animosity toward everybody on this earth for sending me to death row. But I eventually did learn to forgive and forget. But it's so hard to get anybody to listen to you – terribly, terribly hard."

"Time can pass so slowly," he added. "A week can seem like it lasts a whole year. The only way I knew it was Christmas was because we got two desserts. But I feel OK now." He smiled at the reporters. "I've just got a foot that's upsetting me – I've got new shoes on here." He raised one foot to show the new athletic running shoes he was wearing.

Judge Landrith's ruling was especially emotional for Debra Carter's family. They left the courtroom in tears. Debra Carter's mother, Peggy, a still pretty woman in her mid fifties with snow white hair, said, "I want the murder solved more than anybody else. It's almost impossible to let it rest. I live it over and over. Nobody deserved what happened to Debbie." She shook her head. "She was bruised so bad- the only thing that looked like Debbie was her long eyelashes."

"How much do you remember about that time in 1982?" one of the reporters asked.

"The night before the murder," Peggy said, "she came over to my house to do some laundry. She went to school and sometimes worked two jobs. That night she went to sleep on the couch. I remember when she woke up, she crawled into my bed and slept there the rest of the night."

Peggy goes to the cemetery often, but on Memorial Day, she takes the saddle Debbie had for her horse and puts it over the headstone of her daughter's grave.

"Of all my girls, she was the one I worried about the most. I always felt like I had to take up for her. She was just a typical twenty-one year old," Peggy said. "We had our difficulties, but we were close. We were like buddies. I think she was like her sisters – she just wanted to settle down and raise a family."

Peggy said she would be there when the next murder trial happened. "I'll go through it again," she said. "I've got to be there for her. I'd like to put it behind me, but I think about it all the time and I'm going to live it all the time until it's really solved. It's a big puzzle, and all the pieces aren't fitting. I just need some answers. Sometimes I have to get by myself and cry."

One of the jurors, a woman, who sat on the Fritz jury, said she believes that Fritz and Williamson were involved in the Carter murder despite the DNA test results. "I'll go to my grave thinking they were guilty. It wasn't a hard decision for me to make. I can't actually say they pulled the cord around her neck, but I think they were there."

As the two men walked from the courtroom together, escorted by their lawyers, family members and friends, the police surrounded the group warily watching the crowd for any sign of trouble.

Camera crews from ABD, NBC, Oklahoma City's KOCO-TV KWTV and Ada's local KTEN followed this procession to the lodge at Wintersmith Park where a news conference was set up. Fox Television, the Associated Press, and a reporter from the New York office of Reuter's News were also on hand.

At this press conference, the attorneys for these men announced they would be traveling to Oklahoma City that afternoon to address Governor, Frank Keating, and the State Legislature on the need for a fund to compensate people who have proven their innocence and spent time in prison from crimes they did not commit. Oklahoma provides no compensation for wrongfully convicted prisoners.

"It's part of being a civilized society that would provide compensation for these victims," Barry Scheck said.

A barbeque lunch was provided at Wintersmith Lodge for friends and family members. A legendary barbeque restaurant in Ada provided ribs, baked beans and slaw. Reporters roamed through the crowd, filming reunions with the two released men and their friends. Williamson hugged an old friend, "a fishing buddy," he called him. "Hey Craig," he grinned. "You've lost a lot of weight there buddy."

"So have you!"

"But I'm getting ready to fix that," he said as the camera crew focused in on the scene.

That night, a welcome home party for Fritz and Williamson was held at the home of Annette Hudson. Annette and Ron entertained the guests by performing a musical duo. Ron played the guitar, purchased by his sister the day before the release, and Annette accompanied him on the piano.

They sang the classic gospel song, "I'll Fly Away".

CHAPTER TWENTY-FOUR

On April 16, 1999, the day after the release of Williamson and Fritz, the search for Glen Gore began in earnest. The officials at the Joseph Harp Correctional Facility from which Gore had escaped two days before, said they did not know that Gore was a possible suspect in the Carter murder.

Jenese McCoy, assistant to the warden at Joseph Harp in Lexington, Oklahoma, insisted that the Pontotoc County District Attorney's office notified them on March 2, 1999, that Gore was a witness in the Carter murder, but they were never told that he was a suspect.

The prison officials indicated that Gore had earned the privilege of working alone, as it had been more than four years since there were any reports of misconduct on his prison record. He was unsupervised most of the time.

McCoy said nothing unusual was revealed in a search of Gore's personal possessions and nothing in letters he had received that indicated he was planning an escape. McCoy said that he would not have had more than a few dollars in his possession when he escaped.

"How long do you think that boy can live out there in the woods?" the old man asked his younger friend.

"He's a country boy – a while yet, I'd guess."

"When they catch him, he'll be back behind the fence for a long time."

"If they catch him."

"Oh, they'll catch him."

"He have folks around here?"

"Don't know."

"That's what happens most often. They go back home to get help."

"Scene of the crime, you mean?"

"Something like that."

Later, Agnes asked the cook, "Where do you think that boy could be?"

The cook shook his head.

"Well, I'll tell you one thing. I don't want him coming around here asking for help."

"That's not likely to happen. But if it did, you'd be the first one to pack up a lunch for him."

"I would not!" Agnes stood up and squared her shoulders. "I'm not ignorant, you know. I think I can tell a murderer from an innocent man."

"Sure you can," the cook answered.

On Monday afternoon, April 19, 1999, Kenneth Winters, a rancher and quarter horse breeder, was in his barn. He fed and hayed the horses around five p.m. every afternoon. The day had been cool with showers earlier. Heavy gray clouds lingered on the western horizon and Kenneth wanted to finish feeding before the rain began again.

As he went outside to open the stalls, he saw a man running across the pasture toward him. The man was running fast and looking over his shoulder as if he were being followed. As he got closer to the barn, the man raised his hands above his head. "Sir, I'm the man you're looking for."

"I'm not looking for nobody," Kenneth replied.

"You're not afraid of me, are you?"

"I'm real busy right now," Kenneth answered. "I need to get this stock fed before it begins to rain."

"Can I use your phone?"

"Tell you what. You help me carry these buckets and then I'll let you use the phone and call anybody you want to."

The man began filling feed buckets and carrying them to the stalls.

"Much obliged," Kenneth said, after they were finished. "Phone's over there on the wall."

"Need to call my lawyer."

Kenneth nodded. He noticed the fellow's hands were shaking. Whether it was from the chill in the air or because the rain was beginning to fall again, or from exhaustion, he couldn't tell.

Nobody answered any of the numbers he dialed. "What I really need to do," he said, " is to get over to Tupelo. I got some friends there."

It was getting dark.

"Well, I can drive you over there," Kenneth said. "There's a jacket hanging over there by the office. You better put it on."

"Thanks, man," he said.

They got in Kenneth's truck. Kenneth turned on the heater.

"You know who I am, don't you?" the man asked.

"Got a pretty good idea." They turned onto the highway that led to Tupelo, a small town with a population of less than one thousand residents.

"I'm not guilty of killing that girl," Gore said.

"Well, if you're not guilty, then why did you run?"

"I didn't run," he said. " I was in Oklahoma City."

"What were you doing up there in Oklahoma City?"

"I've got a girlfriend up there," Gore answered. "See I've got this pager, and if I need to get back in a hurry, the boss pages me. I guess when I heard they were looking for me I panicked."

It was about twenty miles from Kenneth's ranch to Tupelo. When they neared the town, Gore reached into his pocket and pulled out a roll of bills. Later, Kenneth would say it looked like Gore had between two and three hundred dollars.

"Would you do me a favor?" he asked.

"Sure," Kenneth answered.

"There's a Quick Stop up ahead. I'd appreciate it if you'd go in and buy a six pack of beer and a carton of cigarettes." He handed Kenneth a fifty-dollar bill. "I want my friends to be glad to see me when I get there."

When Kenneth came back with the beer and cigarettes, Gore told him to keep the change. "I'd like to pay you something for your trouble."

"You don't owe me nothing," Kenneth told him as he let him out in front of the small house Gore pointed toward.

On his way back to Ada, Kenneth rolled down the windows in his truck. It was raining hard, but he wanted to eliminate the odor in the truck. It was the smell of fear, whether it was from his passenger or from himself, he didn't know, but one thing he did know was that he was glad he had escaped from what could have been a dangerous situation. His gut feeling was that this guy was going to either turn himself in or get killed by he police and either way, he didn't want anything to do with any part of it.

Two days after Kenneth Winters dropped Glen Gore at the home of Gore's friends – former friends – ex convicts, Gore turned himself in to the Ada Police Department. He was at the home of his brother who lived in Ada.

The next day, Agnes and the cook sat at the counter sharing the newspaper.

The breakfast crowd offered several versions of Gore's surrender to the police.

"Heard he went peaceful like – didn't put up any kind of a fight."

"He called the cops himself. That's what I heard."

"Probably got hungry – on the run for a week or so."

"Probably didn't want to get killed is more like it."

"He's got a better chance of getting killed here in Ada than up there in the pen."

"I hear life's not so bad up there. Anyway, it's gonna be a while before he even gets charged."

"If ever."

"You think he really killed that girl?"

"They got evidence, but nobody around here seems real convinced."

"Guess Ron and Dennis are leaving town."

"My thought is that they better leave quick. Lot's of folks here are mighty suspicious of 'em."

"If it was me, I'd be on the first Greyhound leaving the bus station."

Agnes turned the pages of the newspaper slowly. The cook stood up – stretched and walked back into the kitchen. "Well," she said, "what do you think?"

"What do I think or what do I know?'

"Just tell me what you know."

"One thing I know for certain is that it's a lot easier to get into prison than it is to get out."

"You're beginning to sound like those old guys who come in here every morning to talk."

"You mean a philosopher?"

"Whatever."

Editorials began to appear in newspapers across the county demanding action to allow the indigent defense system to submit evidence from old cases for DNA testing. The indigent defense system was prohibited from getting access to the evidence of old cases.

"We are procedurally barred from doing it once the appeals process has run," Jim Bednar, Director of the Indigent Defense System, said. "There are as many as thirty people wrongfully incarcerated in Oklahoma prisons, but our efforts have been met with resistance from prosecutors as well as the Oklahoma Attorney General, Drew Edmondson. Edmondson indicates that if DNA evidence was made available in all capital crimes, the system would be flooded with frivolous appeals, and the cost to the State would be prohibitive."

Nationally, sixty to seventy people convicted of crimes were later exonerated by DNA testing. Five were from Oklahoma.
In 1987, Ronald Williamson and Dennis Fritz were convicted in Ada for rape/murder and freed after twelve years.

In 1988, Robert Lee Miller, Jr. was convicted for the murders of two elderly women. He was freed ten years later after a DNA test of semen left at the crime semen pointed to another man, already serving a prison sentence for raping two other Oklahoma City women.

In 1993, Timothy Edward Durham was sentenced in Tulsa to 320 years for raping an eleven-year old girl. In 1997, the charge against him was dismissed when a DNA test concluded it wasn't his semen on the girl's bathing suit.

In 1983, Thomas Webb, III, was convicted in the 1982 rape of a Norman woman. He was released in 1996 after it was discovered through DNA testing that it was not his semen found at the crime scene.

"When the FBI conducts DNA testing in rape cases," Bendar said, "the primary suspect is excluded twenty-five percent of the time."

Mary Long, Director of the OSBI's DNA lab, has testified that her lab has excluded rape suspects between twenty-five and thirty percent of the time.

On the other side, Kim Koch, with the OSBI, said, "About one third of the rape suspects plead guilty when they learn DNA samples have been taken and submitted to the OSBI lab."

Although the District Attorney's Council has not taken a position on the indigent defense system, it indicates support, however they have procedural concerns. "It creates a whole new post-conviction process, so you have to be careful about how it works," Suzanne Atwood, Executive Director of the Council said.

Illinois and New York are the only two states that authorize post-conviction DNA testing for inmates and they have the highest number of DNA exonerations.

The concern of Oklahoma Attorney General Drew Edmondson is that many people will believe DNA is magic when it isn't. "You have to look at what it proves," he said. "The case of Loyd Lafevers who was convicted in the 1985 murder of an elderly Oklahoma City woman, recently won a stay of execution because of DNA evidence that proved nothing about his case. DNA evidence proving that blood of Lafevers co-defendant was found on a pair of pants that came out of the co-defendant's house tells us nothing about what Lafevers did." He added that the indigent defense system had not provided him with a name of anyone they think may be wrongfully convicted. Bednar countered by saying that the OIDS can do nothing until he gets the legal authority and resources to examine the evidence.

"Edmondson wants a bill that would allow the indigent defense system to conduct DNA testing without giving the agency legal authority to seek relief in court. He wants his attorneys or perhaps a newly created board to determine whether an appeal would have merit," Bednar said, "however there could be as many as one hundred cases that might warrant DNA testing. The only honest thing to do is to take a hard look at these."

Kevin Acres is President of the Oklahoma Chapter of Amnesty International. In an editorial published in the May, 1999 issue of the Oklahoma Gazette, he said: "Ron Williamson and Dennis Fritz were not arrested until almost six years after the 1982 murder of Debbie Carter. Williamson's only alibi, his mother, had died. They were convicted after an over confident expert inaccurately linked them to physical evidence. Now DNA testing has proven the evidence matches neither Williamson nor Fritz. It incriminates instead a witness whose testimony helped wrongfully convict them. This case suggests that prosecutors are sometimes willing to compromise justice in order to get a conviction. They would risk putting an innocent person behind bars – or even to death – before admitting to the public that there is insufficient evidence to solve a particular crime. The attitude seems to be, "If you can't get the bad guy, get somebody we can sell as the bad guy." A jury will often buy the DA's scenario, even when the evidence is completely circumstantial, or when the entire case hinges on an unreliable "snitch" whose story is part of a deal.

Some people argue that innocent people are infrequently sentenced to death and that it is a risk we have to take in seeking justice for terrible crimes. Look Ron Williamson in the eye and make that argument. If today's shortened appeals process were in effect during his trial, he would already be dead.

On death row, Williamson was warehoused in H-Unit, a modern day dungeon in McAlester. Inmates were locked 23 to 24 hours a day in underground, windowless cells with inadequate ventilation and no natural light. Human Rights Watch is investigating conditions there. Amnesty International and the UN Commission on Human Rights have already condemned H-Unit.

This man spent nine years on death row where his mental health deteriorated and he was denied any medical treatment. Guards taunted him with voices over his cell intercom pretending to be the ghost of Debbie Carter. He sometimes paced naked in his cell without sleeping for days at a time. His attorney, when she protested the physical conditions and his need for medical attention, was told that he was "faking it".

The judge who overturned his conviction, said: "God help us, if ever in this great country we turn our heads while people who have not had fair trials are executed."

God help us, too, if we turn our heads when the political climate makes wrongful convictions more acceptable than prosecutors admitting they don't have a solid case."

There are two powerful arguments for capital punishment. One is that it saves lives, if its deterrence effect is not flawed by sporadic implementation. The other is that it enhances society's valuation of life by expressing proportionate anger at the taking of life. But that valuation is lowered by careless or corrupt administration of capital punishment, which unfortunately is intolerably common.

CHAPTER TWENTY-FIVE

In the December 1, 1999 edition of the Ada Evening News, the headline said, ADA AGAIN NATIONAL NEWS – DATELINE TO AIR STORY OF CARTER MURDER TRIAL. Most of the story was filmed on the day of Fritz and Williamson's release. Scenes of Ada, Fritz and Williamson entering the courtroom in handcuffs, the judge dismissing charges and the reunion of the two men with their family members and friends after twelve painful years were poignant. Camera crewmembers surveyed the crowd gathered at Wintersmith Park Lodge. A long table had been set up in front of the fireplace.

Williamson and Fritz and their attorneys sat behind this table and answered questions from the press. This interview would be replayed on the television news networks across the country that evening.

A few days after the release, Fritz and Williamson flew to New York to appear on the TODAY show. They were, after all, national news and their story struck a nerve with the American public. The school teacher raising his daughter as a single parent, the once heroic baseball player drafted by the Oakland 'A.s' were now gray haired, middle aged men, defeated by a justice system gone terribly wrong.

As they boarded the plane to fly back to Oklahoma, the flight attendant asked for a photo ID. When they shook their heads, the attendant explained about federal regulations requiring passengers to produce a driver's license.

"I haven't had a driver's license for more than twelve years," Fritz said, and then he tried to explain why.

The DATELINE story of the release of Williamson and Fritz aired on December 5, 1999. The overflow crowd of customers at the Parkview the next morning expressed a variety of opinions regarding the program.

"What old Ron said what he did about being about half crooked himself, I thought everybody in this town who knew him would know what he meant."

"At least he admitted that he'd done some things he wasn't very proud of."

"But he didn't murder that girl."

"Said he was moving out of this state. Going to get as far away from Ada and Peterson as soon as he could."

"Being on death row must be a living hell."

"Peterson never backed down. Even when that interviewer kept asking about the plea bargain with Gore."

"And that Holland woman who testified about Williamson threatening to kill his mother."

"She's been in jail so much she has a room reserved with her name on it."

"Peterson said that just because she was in jail a lot didn't mean she was a liar."

"Yeah, right."

"Fritz came across pretty good."

"If it hadn't been for Fritz writing all those letters to get the evidence tested, Ron would be a dead man."

"Said all he wanted was a full apology from Peterson, but he admitted that he didn't expect to get it."

"You heard what Peterson said about that. Said he'd never apologize for doing his job."

"Tell you who I felt sorry for was the Carter girl's mother. Having to go through the whole thing again."

"It may be a long time before that happens."

"Think they'll ever charge Gore?"

The old man shook his head. "Not in my lifetime," he answered.

On February 1, 2000, Senator Frank Leahy of Vermont addressed the Senate on THE GROWING CRISIS IN THE ADMINISTRATION OF CAPITAL PUNISHMENT.

"Mr. President," he began, "I wish to call attention to a growing national crisis in the administration of capital punishment. People of good conscience can and will disagree on the morality of the death penalty. But I am confident that we should all be able to agree that a system that may sentence one innocent person to death for every seven it executes has no place in a civilized society, much less in 21st Century America. But that is what the American system of capital punishment has done for the last 24 years.

A total of 610 people have been executed since the reinstatement of capital punishment in 1976. During the same time, according to the Death Penalty Information Center, 85 people have been found innocent and were released from death row. These are not reversals of sentences, or even convictions on technical legal grounds; these are people whose convictions have been overturned after years of confinement on death row because it was discovered they were not guilty. Even though in some instances they came within hours of being executed, it was eventually determined that, whoops, we made a mistake; we have the wrong person.

What does this mean?

It means that for every seven executions, one person has been wrongly convicted. It means that we could have more than three innocent people sentenced to death each year. The phenomenon is not confined to just a few States; the many exonerations since 1976 span more than 20 different states. And of those who are found innocent, what is the average time they spent on death row, knowing they could be executed at any time? What is the average time they spent on death row before somebody said, we have the wrong person? Seven and a half years.

This would be disturbing enough if the eventual exonerations of these death row inmates were the product of reliable and consistent checks in our legal system, if we could say as Americans, all right, you may spend seven and a half years on death row, but at least you have the comfort of knowing that we are going to find out you are innocent before we execute you. It might be comprehensible, though not acceptable, if we as a society lacked effective and relatively inexpensive means to make capital punishment more reliable. But many of the exonerated owe their lives to fortuity and private heroism, having been denied common sense procedural rights and inexpensive modern scientific testing opportunities, leaving open the very real possibility that there have been a number of innocent people executed over the last few decades who were not so fortunate.

Let me give you a case. Randall Dale Adams. Here is a man who might have been routinely executed had his case not attracted the attention of a filmmaker, Earl Morris. His movie 'The Thin Blue Line' shredded the prosecution's case and cast a national spotlight on Adams's innocence.

Consider the case of Anthony Porter. Porter spent 16 years on death row. He came within 48 hours of being executed in 1998, but was cleared the following year. Was he cleared by the State? No. He was cleared by a class of undergraduate journalism students at Northwestern University, who took on his case as a class project. That got him out. Then the State acknowledged that it had the wrong person, that Porter had been innocent all along.

Now consider the cases of the unknown and the unlucky, about which we may never hear.

Last year, former Florida Supreme Court Justice Gerald Kogan said he had 'no question' that we have, in the past, executed people who either didn't fit the criteria for execution in the State of Florida, or who were factually, not guilty of the crime for which they have been executed. This is not some pie-in-the-sky theory. Justice Kogan was a homicide detective and a prosecutor before eventually becoming Chief Justice.

This crisis has led the American Bar Association and a growing number of State legislators to call for a moratorium on executions until the death penalty can be administered with less risk to the innocent. The Governor of Illinois, George Ryan, has announced his plan to block executions in that State until an inquiry has been conducted into why more death row inmates have been exonerated than executed since 1977 when Illinois reinstated capital punishment. Think of that, more death row inmates exonerated than executed.

I hope that nobody of good faith, whether they are for or against the death penalty, will deny the existence of a serious crisis. Sentencing innocent men and women to death anywhere in our country shatters America's image in the international community. At the very least, it undermines our leadership in the struggle for human rights. But, more importantly, the individual and collective conscience of decent Americans is deeply offended and the faith in the working of our criminal justice system is severely damaged. So the question we should debate is, 'what should be done?'.

Some will be tempted to rely on the States. The U.S. Supreme Court often defers to the 'laboratory of the States' to figure out how to protect criminal defendants.

After 24 years, let's take a look at that lab report.

Illinois has now had more inmates released from death row than executed since the death penalty was reinstated. There have been 12 executions, and 13 times they have said: Whoops, sorry.

Don't pull the switch. We have the wrong person. This has happened four times in the last year alone.

In Texas, the State that leads the Nation in executions, courts have upheld death sentences in at least three cases in which the defense lawyers slept through substantial portions of the trial. The Texas courts said that the defendants in these cases had adequate counsel. Would any one of us, if we were in a taxicab say we had an adequate driver who was asleep at the wheel? What we are saying is with a person's life at stake the defense lawyer slept through the trial, and the Texas courts say that is pretty adequate.

The last few years the States have followed the Federal lead in expanding their defective capital punishment systems, curtailing appeal and habeas corpus rights, and slashing funding for indigent defense services.

The States have had decades to fix their capital punishment systems, yet the best they have managed is a system fraught with arbitrariness and error, a system where innocent people are sentenced to death on a regular basis, and it is left not to the courts, not to the States, not to the Federal Government, but to filmmakers and college undergraduates to correct the mistakes. History shows that we cannot rely on local politics to implement our national conscience on such fundamental points as the execution of the innocent.

Even the Supreme Court, in a 1993 case, could not make up its mind whether the execution of an innocent person would be unconstitutional. Why not ask the people in this nation of a quarter million people whether they think executing an innocent person should be constitutional or unconstitutional. Most citizens would agree that it is unconstitutional, but that doesn't matter, because executing an innocent person is abhorrent and morally wrong. Those of us in this body have the moral duty to express and implement America's conscience. The buck should stop in this Chamber where it always stops in times of crisis.

How do we begin? Two problems in particular require our immediate attention. First, we need to ensure that defendants in capital cases receive competent legal representation at every stage in their case. Second, we have to guarantee an effective forum for death row inmates who may be able to prove their innocence.

In our adversarial system of justice, effective assistance of counsel is essential to the fair administration of justice. It is the principal bulwark against wrongful conviction.

Most prosecutors will tell you they would much prefer to have good counsel on the other side because there is less apt to be reversible error, and there is far more of a chance that you end up with the right decision.

Most defendants who face capital charges are represented by court-appointed lawyers. Unfortunately, the manner in which defense lawyers are selected and compensated in death penalty cases frequently fails to protect the defendant's rights. Some States relegate these cases to grossly unqualified lawyers willing to settle for meager fees. While the Federal Government pays defense counsel $125 an hour for death penalty work the hourly rate in many States is $50 or less, and some States place an arbitrary and usually unrealistically low cap on the total amount a court-appointed attorney can bill.

New York recently slashed pay for counsel in capital cases by as much as 50 percent. They might say they are getting their money's worth if they cut all the money for defense counsel, but the conviction rate is probably going to shoot up. The other thing that will go up is the number of innocent people who will be put to death.

Congress has done its part to make a bad situation worse. In 1996, Congress defunded the death penalty resource centers. This has sharply increased the chances that innocent people will be executed. You get what you pay for. Those who are on death row have found their lives placed in the hands of lawyers who are drunk during the trial, lawyers who never bothered to meet their client before the trial, lawyers who never bothered to read the State death penalty statute, lawyers who were just out of law school and never handled a criminal case and lawyers who were literally asleep on the job. Even some of our best lawyers, diligent, experienced litigators can do little when they lack funds for investigators, experts, or scientific testing that could establish their client's innocence. Attorneys appointed to represent capital defendants often cannot recoup even their out-of-pocket expenses. They are effectively required to work at minimum wage or below while funding their client's defense out of their own pockets.

Let me give three examples of some of the worst things that have happened, but not untypical.

Ronald Keith Williamson. In 1997, a Federal appeals court overturned Williamson's conviction on the basis of ineffectiveness of counsel. The court noted that the lawyer, who had been paid a total of $3,200 for the defense, had failed to investigate and present a fact to the jury. What was that fact? Somebody else confessed to the crime. If I were the defense attorney, I think one of the things I would want to bring to the jury is the fact that somebody else confessed to the crime. Williamson's lawyer didn't bother. Then, two years after the appeals court decision, DNA testing ruled out Williamson as the killer and implicated another man, a convicted kidnapper who had testified against Williamson at trial. Of course he did. He is the one who committed the crime.

Next, lets consider George McFarland. According to the Texas Court of Criminal Appeals, McFarland's lawyer slept through much of his 1992 trial. He objected to hardly anything the prosecution did.

A quote from the Houston Chronicle said: "Seated beside his client, defense attorney, John Benn, spent much of Thursday afternoon's trial in apparent deep sleep. His mouth kept falling open and his head lolled back on his shoulders, and then he awakened just long enough to catch himself and sit upright. Then it happened again. And again. And again.

Every time he opened his eyes, a different prosecution witness was on the stand describing another aspect of the arrest of George McFarland in the robbery killing of grocer Kenneth Kwan. When the state district judge finally called a recess, Benn was asked if he had truly fallen asleep during a capital murder trial. 'It's boring,' the seventy two year old longtime lawyer explained. Court observers said Benn slept his way through the entire trial.

Unfortunately for McFarland, Texas highest criminal court, several of whose members were coming up for reelection, concluded that Benn's behavior constituted effective criminal representation. McFarland is still on death row for a murder he insists he did not commit, on the basis of evidence widely reported by independent observers to be weak.

Reginald Powell was a borderline-mentally retarded man who was 18 at the time of his crime. Powell was eventually executed. Why? Because he accepted his lawyer's advice to reject a plea bargain that would have saved his life.

There were a number of attorney errors at the trial. The advice he received seems to be very bad advice. Some may feel this advice, the advice given to this 18 year old mentally retarded man, was affected by the flagrantly unprofessional conduct of the attorney, a woman twice Powell's age, who conducted a secret jailhouse sexual relationship with him during the trial. Despite the obvious attorney conflict of interest, Powell's execution went ahead in Missouri in 1999.

Can miscarriages of justice happen when defendants receive adequate representation? Yes, it can still happen. That is why it is critical to insure that death row inmates have a meaningful opportunity to raise claims of innocence based on newly discovered evidence, especially if it is evidence that is derived from scientific tests not available at the time of the trial.

More than any other development, improvements in DNA testing have exposed the fallibility of the legal system. In the last decade, scores of wrongfully convicted people have been released from prison, including many from death row, after DNA testing proved they could not have committed the crimes for which they were convicted. In some cases the same DNA testing that vindicated the innocent helped catch the guilty.

It was DNA testing that eventually saved Ronald Keith Williamson's life. He spent 12 years as an innocent man on Oklahoma's death row.

Can you imagine how any one of us would feel, day after day for 12 years, never knowing if we were just a few hours or a few days from execution, locked up on death row for a crime we did not commit?

Some of the major hurdles to post-conviction DNA testing are laws prohibiting introduction of new evidence – laws that have tightened as death penalty supporters have tried to speed executions by limiting appeals. Only two states, Illinois and New York, require the opportunity for inmates to require DNA testing where it could result in new evidence of innocence. Elsewhere, inmates may try to get DNA evidence for years, only to be shut out by the courts and prosecutors.

What possible reason could there be to deny inmates the opportunity to prove their innocence and perhaps even help identify the real culprits through new technologies? DNA testing is relatively inexpensive. But no matter the cost, it is a small price to pay to make sure you have the right person.

The National Commission on the Future of DNA Evidence, a federal panel established by the Justice Department and comprised of law enforcement, judges and scientific experts, issued a report last year urging prosecutors to consent to post-conviction DNA testing, or retesting, in appropriate cases, especially if the results could exonerate the defendant.

By reexamining capital punishment in light of recent exonerations, we can reduce the risk that people will be executed for crimes they did not commit and increase the probability that the guilty will be brought to justice. We can also help to make sure the death penalty is not imposed out of ignorance or prejudice.

Let's not have the situation where, today in America, it is better to be rich and guilty than poor and innocent. That is not equal justice. That is not what our country stands for."

The bill introduced by Mr. Leahy, Mr. Levin, Mr. Feingold, Mr. Monyhihan, and Mr Adada, titled INNOCENCE PROTECTION ACT OF 2000, asked for EXONERATION THE INNOCENT THROUGH DNA TESTING, ENSURING COMPETENT LEGAL SERVICES IN CAPITAL CASES, AND COMPENSATING THE UNJUSTLY CONDEMNED.

CHAPTER TWENTY-SIX

On April 15, 2000, exactly one year after the release of Ronald Williamson and Dennis Fritz, a $100 million wrongful incarceration lawsuit was filed in federal court in Muskogee, Oklahoma.
The Ada Evening news reported that Williamson, 47, and Fritz, 50, are seeking $25 million each in compensatory damages and $50 million in punitive damages.
Listed as defendants in this suit were a variety of people involved in arresting, prosecuting and incarcerating them on rape and murder charges.
"In addition to gaining compensation for their injuries, Mr. Fritz and Mr. Williamson desire to make prosecutors and law enforcement think twice about railroading innocent men," said attorney Richard O'Carroll of Tulsa, Oklahoma. "Dennis Fritz and Ronald Williamson were unconstitutionally arrested, imprisoned, prosecuted and convicted for a murder they did not commit.
District Attorney William Peterson and the other defendants embraced and endorsed the actual murderer and sponsored him as a false witness to convict the innocent plaintiffs," O'Carroll added. "Fritz and Williamson claim in the lawsuit that Glen Gore, 39, who testified against them in the murder case, was the murderer. Gore's DNA matched the DNA collected at the murder scene.
At the time of the Fritz and Williamson trials in 1988, Gore was serving a 40-year prison sentence for kidnapping, burglary and shooting with intent to injure. Gore's convictions all involved an attack on a young woman and her daughter. Peterson dismissed other charges that amounted to 140 years against Gore after he added Gore to the State's witness list for the Fritz and Williamson's trials.
The lawsuit also alleges that Peterson 'shopped for' and eventually embraced numerous unreliable jailhouse snitches, in order to convict these innocent men. Peterson also solicited and presented unreliable and unscientific evidence in his mission to convict. These men also seek damages for abuse of process, false arrest, malicious prosecution, intentional infliction of emotional distress and negligence."
Gerald Adams, spokesman for State Attorney General, Drew Edmondson, said:

"In a wrongful imprisonment lawsuit, the plaintiffs have to show that there was a lack of probable cause at the time. That's going to be very difficult for them to do, because when people allege abuse of process, they must show evil intent."

"Fritz and Williamson claim," O'Carroll stated, " that the defendants did not attempt to determine the actual truth and presented a case based not on fact. They were, rather, motivated by a desire to gain any conviction after the case had been dormant for five years. What the defendants did was to adopt a theory and then construct a case to fit the theory."

Among the defendants are, the District Attorney, Bill Peterson, the State of Oklahoma, the Sheriff and County Commissioners of Pontotoc County, the police chief and the City of Ada, Ada police officer, Dennis Smith, four agents of the OSBI, two deputy sherriffs, former state Corrections Department Directors Gary Maynard, Larry Fields and current Director James Saffle.

"What wasn't concocted was coerced," alleged O'Carroll. "I think there were a lot of men who caused this and it's a perfect example of a case where law enforcement gets an ends-justifies-means mentality."

When interviewed by the Ada Evening News, Peterson said, "In my opinion it's a frivolous lawsuit to attract attention. I'm going to send it to the A.G.'s (Oklahoma Attorney General) office for response. I'm not worried about it."

O'Carroll is one of five attorneys who represent Fritz and Williamson. The other four are Cheryl Pilate, Kansas City, Missouri and Barry Scheck, Peter Nuefeld and Johnnie Cochran, Jr., New York, N.Y.

This suit will cross the desk of Federal Judge Frank Seay, Chief Judge of the Eastern District of Oklahoma," O'Carroll added.

On the morning of April 16, 2000, the old man and his younger friend spread the newspaper across the Formica topped table at the Parkview.

"If you were on the jury in this trial they're talking about here in this newspaper, how much money do you think you'd give those boys?"

"Let me think about that." The younger man pushed his cap up from his forehead. "What do you think a school teacher in Noble, Oklahoma makes?"

"Oh, maybe between $28,000 to $35, 000 a year."

"Whew, that, with some insurance stuff, might come to about $500,000 for the twelve years."

"Course that's before the pain and suffering.'

"What's that?'

"Well, now think about it. You've been convicted. You're gonna spend the rest of your life in the pen. You've lost your family, your kid and you're not guilty. And, besides all that, you haven't had sex for twelve years – at least not with a woman."

"Man that don't make $500,000 sound like much."

"That's what I'm asking – how much is twelve years worth? You've lost your identity. Even if you're free, you can't get a job cause you're a convicted felon. You can't vote. Can't get a credit card cause you haven't had a job for twelve years."

"God damn, what the hell am I gonna do?"

"You're gonna sue the goddamned State and everybody who helped put you away for twelve years."

"What about Williamson?"

"He's gonna do the same thing."

"But, he probably couldn't get a job anyway."

"It don't matter, because he was hurt worse."

"Well, when you put it that way, I guess a hundred million don't hardly seem like it's enough. Do you think they'll get it?"

"Naw, not in my lifetime."

CHAPTER TWENTY-SEVEN

In 2001, Dennis Fritz traveled to Washington D.C. with Barry Scheck where he testified before Congress in support of Mr. Lehy's committee regarding THE INNOCENCE PROTECTION ACT OF 2000.

In his statement, his remarkable plea for fairness from the courts was his hope that no other human being would have to suffer the pain and humiliation he and his family had undergone in the prison system as an innocent man.

In 2002, Ronald Williamson lived in a nursing home near Springfield, Missouri. On Friday and Saturday nights he goes into the city with his guitar and plays the blues.

When interviewed by NPR news he said, "I've got a job at a coffee shop and I'm going to get my driver's license and when I get a car, I can play every night in Springfield. You know, I could play every night."

The Parkview Café closed its doors in 2000. A new business needed the location and the owners sold for a profit. Agnes moved to Tulsa to live with her sister and the cook went to work at the Country Club.

Liquor by the drink, finally came to Ada. The vote was a close one. The Coachlight Club, where the loud music and cheap beer welcomed the rowdy crowds on those weekend nights, dimmed its pink and green lights and disappeared. The building stands empty on the hill waiting for the next tenant.

The garage apartment where Debbie Carter was murdered stood vacant for several years. Marie never had another renter for it. Nobody wanted to live in a place that had witnessed such a terrible crime. She finally had it torn down and the lot cleared. She thought that maybe, someday, she might put a small house on it and plant a flower- bed there.

On August 8, 2002, Special District Judge, John David Miller ordered Glen Gore to stand trial for the 1982 murder of Debra Carter. The order came at the conclusion of Gore's three day preliminary hearing. The prosecutors filed the paperwork to seek the Death penalty. Pontotoc County assistant district attorney, Chris Ross, will prosecute the case, assisted by Richard Wintory from the Attorney General's office in Oklahoma City, the Ada Evening News reported. Bill Peterson recused because of the pending lawsuit against him and numerous others.

On May 12, 2003, jury selection began at the Pontotoc County Courthouse. Gore, 43, was transported from the Oklahoma State Penitentiary at McAlester where he has been detained on a 40-year sentence for first-degree burglary, kidnapping, shooting with intent to kill and feloniously pointing a weapon in 1987.

On May 14, 2003, the trial began. Witnesses testified that when they went to Carter's apartment, December 8, 1982, they found her nude body and writing on a wall, kitchen table and on Carter's back. The writing warned people not to look for the killer and implicated another man in the crime. This writing on the wall said, "Jimmy Smith will be the next to die" while the writing on Carter's back read "Duke Graham." Neither Graham nor Smith were connected to the case, but had had a previous altercation with Gore. Gore was infatuated with Graham's wife, and had hoped to frame Graham to get him out of the way, the assistant district attorney, Richard Wintory said. Gore raped Carter the night she died and decided to kill her because he feared she could identify him as her attacker, Wintory added.

"He tried to kill two birds with one stone," Wintory stated. Three witnesses testified about seeing Gore talking to Carter in a nightclub parking lot within hours of her death. One of those witnesses, Mike Carpenter, said Carter previously told him that she was uneasy around Gore.

Ron West, who knew Gore from the nightclub, said he and Gore ate at an all night diner the night of the murder and then he gave Gore a ride to what he thought was Gore's mother's house Gore's mother lived in a different part of town where West dropped him off. The place where West dropped Gore off was about a mile from Carter's apartment.

"This was likely done to place Gore away from the crime scene," OSBI agent, John Jones, who helped in the investigation in Gore's case, said.

Charlie Carter, Debra Carter's father, who discovered her body, said that he called her name twice and then "I picked her up around the shoulders to see if there were any signs of life."

Seeing that she was dead, he left the apartment and told some people standing outside to call the police.

Tom Bevel, who represented the state, and has investigated more than 500 crime scenes, was asked by Wintory to reconstruct the crime scene in order to determine the type of crime had occurred and if the crime scene could have been staged or tampered with. Bevel who studies existing police and medical examiner records and makes opinions based on his investigations, told the jury that the crime scene displayed evidence of staging and tampering after Carter was murdered. The word "Die" had been written in fingernail polish on the victim's stomach with fingernail polish, and "Duke Gram" had been written in ketchup on her buttocks. The words "Jim Smith next will die" had also been written in fingernail polish on the living room wall, and "Don't look for us or elce" with the obvious misspelling, had been written on the kitchen table.

"A lengthy time frame was spent when words were added in ketchup and fingernail polish," Bevel added. "The nail polish had been written with a plastic applicator brush, and the ketchup had been written with a finger. This is fairly unusual for a murderer to stick around a crime scene. In a high majority of the cases, the offender gets away from the scene immediately."

Bevel also said he discovered evidence that the window in Carter's apartment door was shattered from the inside of the residence. "This was made to look like someone broke in," he said. "Based on the evidence, there were signs of rape in that the clothing had been ripped forcefully. Also evidence of several abrasions and contusions consistent with resistance were evident. Carter was murdered because she could positively identify the rapist. The most common occurrence of this is that the victim has knowledge of the rapist."

Chris Ross presented William Caskey, who worked for the City of Purcell, when Gore had escaped while working as a trustee on a work crew at Purcell on April 14 1999, a day before Fritz and Williamson were released. Caskey said trustees were allowed to work with little supervision. He said on April 14, 1999, he transported Gore to Purcell. "I went to pick up lunch at noon and Glen Gore wasn't there," Caskey said.

David Smith, Gore's attorney, presented testimony from Angela Flores, a longtime friend of Gore's. Flores said she traveled to Purcell on the day he escaped and drove him to her apartment in

Oklahoma City. "Glen Gore called me," she said. "I met him at the sewer plant and we went to McDonald's for breakfast. We got into an argument and then we went to my apartment in Oklahoma City," Flores added. "Then he left to make a phone call and I lost contact with him."

Flores told the prosecutor she didn't want to contact police because they said Gore was armed and dangerous. " I didn't think Glen had a mean bone in his body," she added tearfully.

Smith also presented a local attorney in Ada, David Nimmo, who returned Gore to the prison at Lexington. "Glen Gore and I first met when we both coached tee ball in the mid 1980's," he told Smith.

Nimmo said Gore contacted him from Stonewall and wanted to turn himself in.

"You were aware Glen Gore had escaped and he was considered armed and dangerous?'

"I was not aware that Gore was considered armed and dangerous," Nimmo answered.

On May 23, 2003, it took jurors less than two hours to declare Glen Gore guilty of the murder of Debra Carter.

At the trial, Gore was dressed in a blue shirt with a matching tie and dark gray pants. His hair, still back and thick was trimmed in a conservative cut.

Gore showed little emotion as District Judge Tom Landrith read the jury's verdict at the Pontotoc County Courthouse.

"I strongly feel the verdict was a vindication for Carter's family," said Richard Wintory, senior assistant district attorney of Oklahoma County. "This shows that trials are still about justice"

Debra Carter's mother, Peggy, was relieved with the verdict. " Finally Debbie can rest in peace," she said. " It's hard to believe that it took more than twenty years to find the truth."

"This shows the jury was convinced that the evidence was overwhelming, " said assistant District Attorney Chris Ross. "Although it took 20-plus years, justice finally caught up with Glen Gore."

Ross told jurors it was cruel for the victim to be sexually assaulted with a ketchup bottle after she was beaten and raped. "There is nothing more cruel than to add suffering to someone for enjoyment. We found without a shadow of a doubt that there is no reasonable doubt that Glen Gore is definitely a continuing threat to society. Gore made his choices and you are to determine the fate of his choices. Don't lose sight of what Debra Carter's blood, her body, her injuries are telling you what he chose to do to a family who has endured this pain for all these years and now has to be here today. Their night could not be darker. You lit a candle for them in your verdict today."

Smith, in his closing remarks asked the jury to be merciful to Gore.

Prosecutors presented testimony from persons that witnessed previous crimes for which Gore had been convicted. Gwen Lane and retired Ada Police officer Rick Carson related an incident when Gore kidnapped Lane and her 3-year old daughter in Ada after their divorce. Lane was married to Gore for eleven months in 1985.

"It wasn't a good relationship, it was a controlling relationship," she told Assistant District Attorney for Oklahoma County, Lynn Loftis, who also represented the state. Lane said Gore broke into her apartment twice after their divorce.

Lane said Gore first broke into her apartment and held a knife to her throat. Lane said a friend managed to pull her from her apartment as Gore was trying to keep her inside.

One year later, Lane said, Gore broke into her apartment again and held her and her daughter hostage on February 22, 1987, while Ada Police Officers negotiated outside. "I truly thought we were going to die," she said. "I had accepted the fact that I was going to die. I didn't want him to kill me in front of my daughter."

One of the police officers said that he was shot by Gore during the kidnapping incident, and another shot by Gore narrowly missed an assisting officer. "I was shining my flashlight at the ground and a gunshot came from inside the house. I felt my face stinging."

Gore was convicted for first-degree burglary and assault and battery with a dangerous weapon for this incident.

Prosecutors also heard testimony from Deborah Newsom, who dated Gore for four months beginning in February 1983, just two months after Carter's death. Newsom told Loftis that Gore had continually threatened and beat her. She also said he raped her on the side of a highway near Durant, while her 6-year old son was in the vehicle.

Defense attorneys presented victim impact evidence from Gore's family members, including his mother, Louise Gore, and his sister, Connie Mann. Their testimony presented Gore as a loving uncle and brother, whose father was never in the home. Gore's family said he enjoyed working with children and was always willing to help his family members.

"We never had a home," said Louise Gore. "Glen's father was violent and he was never around." She said Gore was involved as a Kiwanis Little League coach.

"Glen was en energetic child that made everyone laugh," his sister Connie Mann said. "He had lots of friends."

While satisfied that Gore will head to death row, Carter's family is still pained by Debbie Carter's death 20 years later.

Charlie Carter said he had nightmares for years after her death and has a difficult time feeling any joy.

"Since then, I can't explain it, but something doesn't feel right," he said in a statement read by prosecutor Lynn Loftis. He said he was too emotional to read the statement himself.

Other family members shared his grief. "This has put a hole in all of our hearts," Darla Tatum, one of Carter's two sisters said.

On June 24, 2003, Judge Tom Landrith issued the death penalty at the Pontotoc County Courthouse for Glen Dale Gore, 43, for the murder of Debra Sue Carter. Ten days later, Gore was delivered to death row at Oklahoma State Penitentiary at McAlester.

Debra Carter's mother, Peggy, said, "I plan to go to the execution and I plan to be on the front row. He'll die easier than my little girl did."

"I feel like the death penalty is not something you celebrate, but based on the viciousness of the murder and the facts of this case, it was warranted," Assistant District Attorney Chris Ross, who also represented the State said.

Gore's attorney, David Smith, and Gore remained silent when asked by Judge Landrith if they had anything to say.

The case of Williamson and Fritz against the State of Oklahoma and others in requesting compensation for time served was finally settled in 2003. The court sealed the amount and terms of the settlement.

Gore's scheduled execution on September 10, 2003, was postponed because his notice to appeal the judgment and sentence was filed on August 1, 2003.

On December 9, 2004, Ronald Keith Williamson died of cirrhosis of the liver. He was 51 years old.

His obituary, which appeared in the New York Times by Jim Dwyer stated:

"Ronald Keith Williamson, who left his small town in Oklahoma as a high school baseball star with hopes of a major league career but was later sent to death row and came within five days of execution for a murder he did not commit, died on Saturday at a nursing home near Tulsa. He was 51 years old.

The cause was cirrhosis of the liver, which he learned he had six weeks ago, his sister, Annette Hudson said.

Mr. Williamson's early life appeared charmed. As a pitcher and catcher in Ada, he twice led his high school teams to the championship of a state where another native son, Mickey Mantle, enjoyed the status of near deity. The Oakland Athletics picked Mr. Williamson in the second round of the 1971 amateur draft. After six years in the minor leagues, Mr. Williamson saw his career end because of arm injuries. He returned to Oklahoma and worked at a sales job, but began to show signs of a mental illness that was eventually diagnosed as bipolar disorder. His marriage, to a former, Miss Ada, broke up. He returned to his mother's home and slept 20 hours a day on the couch, Ms. Hudson said, afraid of his old bedroom.

In late 1982, a waitress Debbie Sue Carter, 21 was found raped and killed in her apartment in Ada. The case remained open until 1987, when a woman who had been arrested for passing bad checks told the police that she had heard another prisoner discussing the killing. The man, she said, was Mr. Williamson who had been in the jail for kiting checks.

Mr. Williamson was charged with the killing. So was a second man, Dennis Fritz, a high school science teacher who had been one of Mr. Williamson's few friends when he returned to town after his baseball career ended.

The evidence, the authorities said, consisted of 17 hairs that matched those of Mr. Williamson and Mr. Fritz, and the account provided by the woman who said she had heard Mr. Williamson confess.

A second jailhouse informer later stepped forward to buttress the case against Mr. Fritz.

Mr. Williamson and Mr. Fritz were tried separately and found guilty. Mr. Fritz was sentenced to life in prison, and Mr. Williamson – who had not received his psychiatric medicines for months before the trial and shouted angrily at the Prosecution witnesses – was sentenced to die.

Mr. Williamson later said the prison guards taunted him over an intercom about Ms. Carter's murder. In September 1994, when all of his state appeals had been exhausted, he was taken to the warden's office and told that he would be executed on September 24. He recalled filling out a form that directed his body to be returned to his sister for burial.

A team of appellate lawyers, however, sought a writ of habeas corpus from Judge Frank Seay of the Federal District Court, arguing that Mr. Williamson had not been competent to stand trial and that his lawyer had not effectively challenged the hair evidence or sought other suspects. Judge Seay granted the request five days before Mr. Williamson was scheduled to die.

In 1998, lawyers from the Innocence Project at the Benjamin C. Cardozo School of Law in New York arranged DNA tests for Mr. Williamson and Mr. Fritz. They showed that neither man had been the source of the semen or hair collected from the victim's body.

Another man, Glen D. Gore, has since been convicted of the killing and sentenced to die for it.

Mr. Williamson and Mr. Fritz were freed in April 1999. On a visit that spring to New York, they took a tour of Yankee Stadium, and Mr. Williamson wandered along the sparkling outfield grass.

"I just got a taste of how much fun they were having up here," he said.

Besides Ms. Hudson, another sister, Renee Simmons of Allen, Texas, survives.

The two men later won settlements for their convictions. But Mr. Williamson continued to be troubled by his psychiatric problems, Ms. Hudson said. Last year, however, he participated in a one-mile march, making an appeal to the governor of Illinois to commute the sentences of death row prisoners in that state.

Mr. Williamson was buried in Memorial Park Cemetery in Ada, Oklahoma."

It was not until April 15, 2005, that the Oklahoma Court of Appeals heard oral arguments in the case of Glen Gore.

Gore's appellate attorney, Gloyd McCoy of Norman, Oklahoma and Robert Whitaker of the Oklahoma Attorney General's Office, presented their oral arguments before the four sitting members of Oklahoma's Court of Criminal Appeals.

Whitaker said the evidence of Gore's guilt in this case is substantial, but McCoy insisted that the real issue before the Court is whether Gore's initial trial was conducted fairly. "The trial court refused to allow the defense to present evidence about Fritz and Williamson. Gore's original defense team requested permission to tell the jury two other men had previously been convicted of the same crime and that one of them, Williamson, had been sentenced to death for it. Gore's attorneys also wanted to argue that Fritz and Williamson had, in fact, committed the crime," McCoy added.

Whitaker argued that the original trial judge was correct in not allowing the evidence by saying, "This is about Gore, not about Fritz and Williamson. The defense wanted to say they were involved when the forensics were dramatically opposite that conclusion."

When interviewed by a reporter from the Ada Evening News, Pontotoc County Assistant Attorney Chris Ross said, "It's an interesting case because, as a general rule, evidence that someone other than the defendant committed the crime is not admissible unless that other person committed some overt act proving they were involved. Clearly, that was not present in this case. Gore's trial was fair and I'm not concerned about the prospect of the case being sent back for retrial."

"I don't see the court reversing this conviction. Judge Landrith tried an extremely clean case. He is an exceptional trial judge. The law and the facts of the case are four-square against Gore," said Richard Wintory, who assisted the Ada District Attorney.

"I'm not able to gauge how the Court of Criminal Appeals judges will vote," McCoy stated. " However I am pleased with the way things went. I felt the questions asked by the panel of judges were "leaning our way." McCoy, who has handled more than 300 appeals and more than 10 capital appeals, predicted that the Court will overturn the sentence and send the case back to be retried. "I'm optimistic that the case will be reversed."

On August 30, 2005, the headline in the Daily Oklahoman read:

DEATH ROW INMATE GETS NEW TRIAL FROM APPEAL

DNA brought conviction in a 1982 slaying.

In ordering a new trial, the Court of Criminal Appeals said, "As early as 1915, this court held that a defendant may show, by any legal evidence, that some other person committed the crime with which he is charged, and that he is innocent of any participation in it." Gore was tried four years after Williamson and Fritz were released from prison because of DNA testing. The Court said that results of this testing showed that sperm found on the victim was not Williamson's or Fritz's, but was that of Gore; however Gore's claim that the trial judge's ruling that he could not submit evidence to the jury that others might have committed the crime denied him due process and the right to put on a defense.

The decision of the court was unanimous with Charles S. Chapel, Presiding Judge, Gary L. Lumpkin, Vice presiding Judge, Charles A. Johnson, Judge and Arlene Johnson, Judge concurring. Chris Ross, assistant district attorney in Ada, when asked by a reporter from the crowd of people gathered in the court house yard, what would happen next, replied that the district attorney's office would prosecute Gore again.

"When?" one reporter shouted but his question went unanswered.

CHAPTER TWENTY-EIGHT

On June 7th, 2006, 85 potential jurors reported for possible service in the retrial of Glen Gore. As the jury selection began Richard Wintory, lead prosecutor said, "We want folks that get along with each other, are respectful of others, willing to listen, enough experience in life and their values and beliefs to be able to make decisions. They need to have enough sense of duty to be willing to decide a hard thing for people. We don't have Debbie Carter here to speak, that's intangible, the defendant is present and that is something the jury can see."

Wintory had returned to Ada from his position as a prosecutor in Tucson, Arizona, to help prosecute Gore. He had promised the family of Debbie Carter that he would prosecute Gore again because of the emotionally charged situation. Several of Carter's relatives planned to be in the courtroom every day of the trial, including Carter's mother, Peggy. "We're going to ask for the death penalty again," she said. "I hope we get it and I just hope this will be the last time. I can't handle any more."

David Smith, attorney for the defense said, "We are looking for people who don't have their minds made up, that will listen and be fair. I'm glad to have a second chance to defend Glen."

One issue prospective jurors were questioned about was whether or not they could decide punishment if the defendant were found guilty of first-degree murder. The three punishment options for a guilty verdict are, death, life in prison without the possibility of parole or life in prison with the possibility of parole. Another concern for the prosecutors was whether anyone harbored any outrage over the taxpayer burden of the expenses of the civil trial that occurred after the Fritz and Williamson cases were dismissed.

Although attorney Mark Hendrickson, El Reno, had been appointed by the Oklahoma Indigent Defense System to represent Gore, Hendrickson told the court that Gore had expressed a very strong preference for David Smith, who had represented him in the original trial, to remain his counsel. "I have the right to choose who represents me," Gore said. "It's my life and I feel more comfortable with David. I'll represent myself if it's not this guy."

Chris Ross, Assistant District Attorney, asked the court if O.D.I.S. was going to pay for Smith's attorney fees and the O.D.I.S. declared that they would not, but believed the local court fund should. Actually, Smith agreed to represent Gore free of charge.

Defense attorneys David D. Smith, Norman, and Cheryl Ramsey, Stillwater, had requested that there be no surprise witnesses, no photographs other than what had been presented during the previous trial for Gore. They also requested that Gore be seated near the jury. It was also agreed that the bulk of the case would be as before and that the original trial transcript would serve as disclosure.

The prosecuting attorneys, Richard Wintory and Chris Ross, agreed to these requests as well as the defense request that Gore be housed in the county jail in Ada for the duration of this re-trial rather than daily transporting him the Oklahoma State Penitentiary at McAlester.

At the time that Gore was charged with the murder of Debra Carter tried and sentenced to death in May of 2002, he was serving a 40-year sentence on charges including first degree burglary, shooting with intent to injure, feloniously pointing a weapon, kidnapping and the felony of carrying a firearm. Gore escaped from a Cleveland County prison in 1999, apprehended and sentenced to five more years.

Seven witnesses gave occasionally fuzzy testimony, trying to recall the events of twenty-four years ago when Debra Sue Carter was brutally raped, sodomized and murdered in her garage apartment. This was the fourth trial in this 1982 murder case and much of the testimony and the witness statements followed the previous trials.

Toni Ramsey testified that on the night of the murder, she saw Carter angrily pull away from Gore after dancing with him at the club. She said that later she saw them together in the parking lot by Carter's car.

Tommy Glover also said he saw the pair in the club's parking lot and Carter pushed Gore away.

Gina Vietta, who was the last known person to have talked to Carter, repeated her previous testimony about the phone call she had from Carter at approximately 2:30 a.m. when she said that someone was in her apartment and she was uncomfortable with him. Carter then asked Vietta to come over and pick her up, but then there was a muffled sound as if someone had covered the mouthpiece. After a few minutes Carter called her again and said, "never mind" but asked her to call the next morning to wake her up for work.

Ron West testified about giving Gore a ride to the Coachlight and later that night drove him to Oak Street where Gore told him he could walk to his mother's house.

Much of the testimony centered on graphic photos and details of how Debbie Carter was killed. The Carter family members left the courtroom when these photos were shown to the jury.

Dennis Smith, former Ada Assistant Police Chief told jurors how his team gathered evidence of clothing, hair and ketchup and shampoo bottles, for analysis. On cross examination, however he admitted that investigators should have dusted Carter's bathroom for fingerprints because the washcloth that gagged her, along with a bottle of shampoo may have come from there.

The medical examiner, Dr. Fred Jordan, was unavailable to testify but his testimony from Gore's first trial was read to the jury. "There were many defensive bruises on her arms, numerous abrasions and bruising. She had been raped, beaten, and anally raped prior to her death from asphyxiation. A washcloth had been shoved forcefully into her throat and a ligature tightened around her neck. A ketchup bottle top was deep inside her rectum."

Forensic experts, called by the prosecution, stated that the hair evidence was compared to Carter, Gore, Dennis Fritz, Ron Williamson, and a third suspect, Ricky Simmons and was inaccurately identified as coming from Fritz and Williamson who were convicted of Carter's murder. "What is so shocking," Wintory said, "is that the error rate in the microscopic analysis done in the 80's was subjective. The analyst was influenced by being told who the suspects were."

Gore's defense attorneys argued that Gore and Carter had consensual sex at some point before her death, although Gore told police in 1999 that there was no reason why his semen would have been found on Carter's body.

Tom Bevel, a crime scene investigator testified that he believed some of the events and details surrounding the 1982 rape and killing of Debra Carter were staged.

"The word 'die' written in nail polish on Carter's chest, the name 'Duke Graham' on her back in catsup and 'don't look for us or elce' in the kitchen with catsup were an attempt by the killer to misdirect investigators."

He also stated that the glass door was broken to make it look as if there was a forced entry when it was actually broken from inside the apartment.

Assistant District Attorney Chris Ross introduced a tape made of Glen Gore's interview by Wes Edens in 1999. On the tape, Gore talked about his relationship with Debra Carter since school days. He said he had been "skinny dipping" with her and others, including her boyfriend and had been horseback riding with her in the past. Edens testified that Gore had been reluctant to answer his questions and had to ask him several times to be sure Gore understood he was asking if Gore had been intimate with Carter the night of her death. Gore admitted to being intimate with her within the last two or three months prior to her death, but would not admit to having sex with her that night.

Danny Barrett, detective, was sent to canvas the neighborhood the afternoon following Carter's death, but finding no witnesses, had nothing to report.

Jerry Peters testified his role in the investigation included obtaining the finger and palm prints from the victim at the medical examiner's office as well as when her body was exhumed in 1985.

Mark Barrett, a criminal defense lawyer from Norman had worked for the O.I.D.S. in the mid to late 1990's. He was involved in the effort to free Williamson and testified that it was his belief that Williamson's mental illness was exacerbated by the torture in prison by the guards and the denial of medical attention which resulted in his not receiving a fair trial. The 10th Circuit Court of Appeals offered the opinion that Williamson's prior history of mental illness could have made a case for a lesser charge of manslaughter, which would not have carried the death sentence.

Many of the witnesses for the defense had to be prompted by the police records and statements in the press to recall the events of twenty years ago. The defense focused much of their questioning on Ron Williamson and Dennis Fritz.

Gary Rogers, who was an agent for the Oklahoma State Bureau of Investigation in 1982, testified that in one interview he had with Williamson said, "I went to the Coachlight and saw a pretty girl there and I wanted to follow her home. I had a dream where I tied a rope around this girl's neck and stabbed her." However, when questioned by the prosecution, Rogers said that Williamson did not make a reference to Carter and a rope was not found at the crime scene and Carter was not stabbed. Rogers had to refer to his police records several times and frequently said that he could not remember specific events exactly.

David Nimmo, an Ada attorney, had known Gore when they both coached little league baseball teams in the 1980's. He stated that he was surprised when he had a phone call from Gore in 1999 after he had escaped from a Lexington prison work program when he heard that DNA evidence had freed Williamson and Fritz. "I didn't believe it was him when he identified himself," Nimmo said. "He was calling from a residence in Stonewall, Oklahoma and wanted to turn himself in."

"Debra Sue Carter was violently raped and murdered by one person, Glen Gore," Special Prosecutor Richard Wintory said in his closing remarks to the jury. "Her body is the evidence."

Gore had been sworn in without the presence of the jury as a formality to waive his right to testify in his own behalf by pleading the Fifth Amendment.

The prosecution rested and the defense offered no rebuttal. The jury deliberated six hours. There were armed guards inside the Pontotoc County Courtroom as Judge Thomas Landrith read the guilty verdict reached by the eight woman, four man jury. Gore's mother wept while holding hands with her daughters.

Carters mother, Peggy stayed in another room until she was told of the verdict. Her granddaughter came to give her the news. "When my granddaughter came in and said they said guilty, I nearly lost it then because it was such a relief," she said. "We thought last time was the end. All I want now is justice and that can happen when Gore gets the death penalty." After a long pause, she said, " I do feel sorry for his mother. I really do."

The jury began their deliberations in the penalty phase mid afternoon on Thursday, June 22, 2006. After ten and one half hours – at 2:30 a.m. Friday, Judge Landrith brought the jury back into the courtroom. The jury foreman said they were deadlocked at 11 to 1 in favor of the death penalty and the foreman asked for five more minutes. The judge refused and pronounced the sentence himself. He sentenced Gore to life without the possibility of parole.

Many of the jurors stayed in the courtroom to talk to Debbie Carter's mother, Peggy. Several cried with her. "I'm right where I was twenty-four years ago," she said. "Lots of people will say that it's ok if he gets life, but it's not. It will never let us put Debbie to rest. All I wanted was justice but------------------------**THERE WAS JUSTICE FOR NONE**

ACKNOWLEDGMENTS

I would like to thank the children of the late Michael Cauthron for permission to use their late father's remarkable poems from his collection, " Bedrock – Images From The Wayside", U.S. District Judge Frank Seay and U.S. District Judge Jim Payne for their interest and support of this project and the staff of the Ada Evening News.